Seance and Sensibility

A Tearoom Mystery
Kirsten Weiss

misterio press

Copyright

COPYRIGHT © 2025 BY Kirsten Weiss

All rights reserved.

No part of this publication may be reproduced, distributed, or transmitted in any form or by any means, including photocopying, recording, or other electronic or mechanical methods, without the prior written permission of the publisher, except as permitted by U.S. copyright law. For permission requests, contact kweiss2001@kirstenweiss.com.

The story, all names, characters, and incidents portrayed in this production are fictitious. No identification with actual persons (living or deceased), places, buildings, and products is intended or should be inferred. AI has not been used in the conceptualization, generation, or drafting of this work.

NO AI TRAINING: Without in any way limiting the author's [and publisher's] exclusive rights under copyright, any use of this publication to "train" generative artificial intelligence (AI) technologies to generate text is expressly prohibited. The author reserves all rights to license uses of this work for generative AI training and development of machine learning language models.

Book Cover by Dar Albert

misterio press / ebook edition 2025

Visit the author website to sign up for updates on upcoming books and fun, free stuff: KirstenWeiss.com

Special Offer!

THANK YOU FOR BUYING *Séance and Sensibility*! I have a free gift if you'd like to read more light paranormal mystery! You can download *Fortune Favors the Grave*, a novella in my Tea and Tarot series, FREE right here —> Get the Book.

Will Abigail become a hostage to fortune?

Independent Abigail Beanblossom finally has the tearoom of her dreams, even if it is chock full of eccentric Tarot readers. But when her Tarot reading business partner, Hyperion Night, becomes embroiled in a rival's murder, Abigail discovers that true partnership is about more than profit and loss.

Escape into this hilarious mystery today!

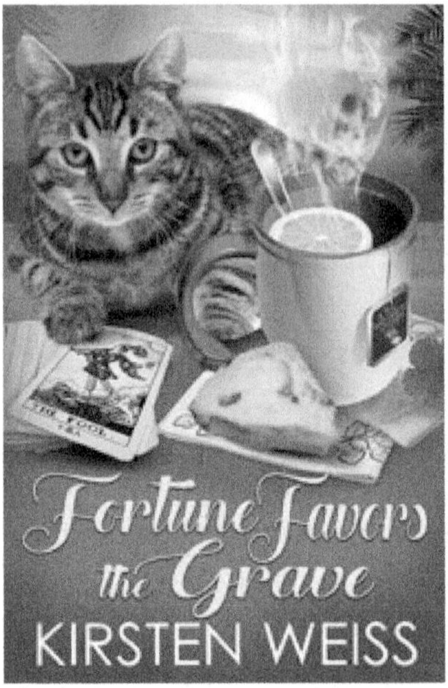
Fortune Favors the Grave
KIRSTEN WEISS

Contents

About the Book	VII
Chapter 1	1
Chapter 2	11
Chapter 3	16
Chapter 4	24
Chapter 5	31
Chapter 6	38
Chapter 7	43
Chapter 8	52
Chapter 9	58
Chapter 10	67
Chapter 11	72
Chapter 12	78
Chapter 13	84
Chapter 14	89
Chapter 15	95
Currant Scones	100
Beanblossom's Swag Shop!	102
More Kirsten Weiss	103
Introducing the UnTarot App: Step into the Enchantment of Kirsten Weiss's Mystery School Series!	106

| About the Author | 109 |
| Other misterio press books | 111 |

About the Book

IN THE BEACH TOWN of San Borromeo, (patron saint of heartburn suffers), Abigail and Hyperion have brewed more than just the perfect cup of Darjeeling. Their latest endeavor? Hosting a séance for the local Jane Austen fan-fic group in their tea and Tarot room.

But when the candles flicker and plunge the tearoom into darkness, the gathering takes a turn to sense and suspicion. Because when the lights come on, a guest is dead. With Abigail's grandfather at the top of the suspect list, the situation brews into a real problem.

With Abigail's grandfather in the hot seat as a suspect, our amateur detectives must sift through the clues faster than Abigail can pour a cup of Earl Grey. Will they manage to read the signs before the killer serves them their last cup of tea?

Join Abigail and Hyperion in *Séance and Sensibility*, a new novella in the Tea and Tarot mystery series. In this culinary cozy mystery, only one thing is certain: the truth will be as hard to catch as the perfect Mr. Darcy.

Scone recipe in the back of the book!

Chapter 1

"It is a truth universally acknowledged, that Jane Austen pairs well with tea and scones."

My assertion was both wildly true and wildly false. Scones weren't a part of Austen's novels—at least not the type of scones we were familiar with today. Baking powder hadn't been invented yet.

Still. Jane Austen and scones was a no-brainer.

One elbow on Beanblossom's hostess stand, Hyperion shot me a droll look. "How long did it take you to come up with that one?" He fluttered an antique-looking fan, ruffling the silky green scarf around his neck.

At the worst of times, Hyperion looked like a male model, ebony of hair, lean of build, dark of gaze. His cheekbones were the envy of many a San Borromeo woman, and not a few of the men, too.

"How long did it take you to learn to run a séance?" I countered.

Hyperion was a master Tarot reader. He'd even published a book on the topic. I managed the tearoom. Together, we'd come up with a combo even more impossible to resist than Jane Austen and scones – Beanblossom's Tea and Tarot.

"I'm not *running* the séance," he corrected. "I'm *facilitating*. Everyone has the power to reach out and touch the departed. It's one of the many benefits of being a living, breathing human."

"Uh, huh." I scanned the tearoom. Antique drawings of herbs hung from the walls. Books on tea and fortune telling lined a shelf against the brick wall. Single-serving teapots lined the elegant reclaimed-wood counter, with its white quartz top.

It was a balmy September, and I was looking forward to decorating for Halloween. I was also looking forward to getting my boyfriend, Brik, back. He was in Alaska working on a construction project for a friend and would return next week.

In the meantime, I had a séance to keep me warm tonight.

All the tables were covered in white cloths, though only one round table—in the center of the room—was occupied. Five people in various states of casual dress eyed the tiers of currant scones and other Jane Austen-themed goodies.

"Your séance is going to be a little tight," I told him. "That's a table for six. With the person you're waiting on plus you, that makes seven."

"*Our* séance, and I want things cozy," Hyperion said. He toyed with the scarf, knotting and unknotting it, then threw it over his shoulder.

"Nice scarf," I said, since he was obviously dying for me to comment.

"Thanks." His coffee eyes glittered. "It's Versace. Vintage."

"Seriously?" I asked. "Where'd you get that?" Beanblossom's had come a long way since our early days. But neither of us had reached blowing-money-on-designer-duds levels of profit.

"Oh." Hyperion fluttered his fan. "*You* know, the usual place one acquires a classic piece of fashion history."

Whatever. "And you *do* know that fan-fic refers to fan fiction, not fans of… fans?"

"Natch." My partner straightened off the hostess stand and snapped his fan shut. "I'm setting the mood with props. The costume shop wanted a mint for a full Regency-era costume."

I glanced at the light switch near the blue front door. It was September and sunset on the California coast wasn't until 7:30, fifteen minutes away. I hoped the tearoom would be dark enough once we turned off the chandeliers overhead.

Normally, we closed at five. But this was a special event—a séance for a local Jane Austen Fan-fic group.

"No offense, but are you sure you can pull this off?" I whispered. Hyperion had been drafted into running the séance, but he was no more a medium than I was. He was, however, an expert on Tarot, which he'd assured me was close enough.

"Of course. I told them my qualifications—"

"Which are?" I canted my head.

"Puh-lease. I've attended dozens of séances. Some of my best friends are mediums. They've told me how it's done. And I never promised the ghost of Jane Austen."

The blue front door rattled. Hastily, I turned and opened it.

My grandfather stood on the brick sidewalk. A black velvet double-breasted jacket strained against his gut. Greenish button-up breeches—it was impossible to call them slacks—were tucked into a pair of black high boots.

I gaped. "Ah..."

He doffed his tall, conical hat, exposing a wig of curling white hair. "Good evening, granddaughter."

I blinked. What was my grandfather doing here? And dressed like a regency dandy?

Hyperion's brown eyes widened. "O.M.G."

"Like it?" Gramps asked.

"I'm *loving* it." My partner whacked his fan on the edge of the hostess stand for emphasis.

"Are the others here?" Gramps ambled past me and into the tearoom.

"Frank?" a slim blond man at the table shouted. He hooted. "Where did you get that outfit?"

The blond man wore all black, even his button-up shirt, its collar open beneath his jacket. The fabric looked expensive and made him look sallow, like a vampire in a cable TV show—the kind that came with parental warnings.

"Like it?" My grandfather held his arms wide as he moved to join the others.

"What the...?" He *couldn't* be here for the séance. This was a *fan-fic* group. "Gramps, do you know these people?"

"Only online," he said over his shoulder. "They're part of my fan-fic group."

"Your..." My brain melted and slowly reconstituted itself. "You write... Jane Austen fan fiction?"

"Obvs, he does." Hyperion brandished his fan. "Keep up."

My jaw slackened. This was impossible. My grandfather had raised me after my parents' abandonment—a villainous act worthy of Jane Austen's Mr. Wickham. Gramps and I were *close*.

I knew about his love of cherry pipe tobacco and lasagna and military history. Sure, classic novels lined his bookshelf. But never had I known him to hold any creative writing aspirations. He would have told me if he had.

So why *hadn't* he?

I turned to close the door. My grandfather's hobby was a question for another time. We had a séance to run.

Across the street, a figure scraped a walker up the slope to a burger joint. That restaurant's door opened outward—tricky if you used a walker.

I trotted across the narrow road. "Allow me." Edging around the gray-haired woman, I opened the door.

She nodded. "Thank you, young lady. I'd tell you not to get old," she said dryly, "but it beats the alternative."

I watched her hobble inside, then I stepped back onto the brick sidewalk. From my vantage on the hillside, I could see the restaurants edging the Pacific, their lights twinkling havens. I could see the horizon, bands of blue-gray darkening to purple. I could see the gunmetal fogbank, joining ocean to sky.

Across the street was my own haven, its walls swirls of white stucco shining in the dimming light. Lights from our chandeliers glowed faintly through the drawn curtains. The wooden sign that my grandfather had made hung above the sidewalk. *Beanblossom's Tea and Tarot*.

Once again I marveled at how lucky I was, doing what I loved in such a beautiful spot. And I sent a silent *thank you* to whoever, or whatever, might be listening.

I strode across the street and entered the tearoom. The other guests had gathered around my grandfather, standing beside the central table.

"I thought I'd come as Mr. Bennet," Gramps was saying.

"You're perfect," a twenty-something woman squealed, clapping her hands together. Her black t-shirt proclaimed, *Trust Me, I'm an Actor*. She'd piled her dark hair on her head in a loose bun and painted her thick eyeliner on Cleopatra-style. "I'm Lizzy."

"Thanks," my grandfather told her. "It's nice to meet you in person."

"Indeed," a silver-haired woman purred. She wore an expensive looking pale-blue tunic top and matching slacks. The woman stroked the sleeve of his jacket possessively. "This is quality fabric. Where did you find it?" She pressed a hand to her chest. "I'm Kathy, by the way."

"A friend of mine works at the local theater," Gramps said. "It's a loaner."

"Very nicely done, Mr. Beanblossom." The older woman's lips curved. "And it's *very* nice to finally meet you in person."

"A shame it had to be during a *séance*," a tall, dark-haired man in navy blue growled.

Kathy stiffened. "No one forced you to come, *Derek*."

Derek's chiseled jaw tightened. "The only reason any of you are here is because of my company."

"Let it go." The fashionable blond vampire clapped Derek's shoulder.

Derek turned his dark gaze on him. "I don't let things go. Ever."

The blond man dropped his hand. His shoulders sagged beneath his ebony jacket.

Kathy sniffed. "You'll have to let it go in this case, Derek. *I'm* going to buy that letter."

"Do you think so?" A crooked smile played about Derek's thin lips. "Why do you think I'm here?"

"Why *are* you here?" Lizzy snapped.

"To make sure no deals are done behind my back." Derek glared.

"And because he wanted to see a real-life outgrowth of his company," another man said quickly. He was dark-haired and diminutive, by which I mean he wasn't much taller than me, and I got called *elf* a lot. Mostly by Hyperion.

Gramps' expression turned misty. "I'd love to just see the letter."

"Letter?" I asked, still reeling over my grandfather's secret hobby. He was a retired CPA. Logical. Utilitarian. He spent his retirement selling horseradish at the farmer's market.

Though he did have a duck for a pet.... I should have suspected there was more whimsy in Gramps than met the eye.

"A letter from Jane Austen to a girl in Steventon about a poem the girl had written." My grandfather adjusted his tall black hat. "I wonder what advice she gave?"

"You don't have to wonder," the blond man said. "Come over and see it. I haven't sold the letter yet."

"You're Giorgi then?" Gramps stuck his hand out, and the two men exchanged grips. "How'd you get your hands on one of Jane's letters?"

"Good question," Derek said.

Giorgi's eyes narrowed, then he refocused on Gramps. "The letter is what sparked my love of Jane Austen," Giorgi said. "My grandmother was a pack rat—she kept boxes and boxes of old family documents, most of them worthless. After she died, I spent weeks going through them, and I found the letter. I couldn't believe it at first. I'd never read any Jane Austen, but of course I knew who she was. Then I started doing research on Jane, trying to verify if the letter could possibly be real. It all checked out. And of course I read her books."

"And so you started writing fan fiction?" I asked him.

"And so he *failed* to start a fan fiction site," Derek said.

Giorgi's skin mottled. A muscle pulsed in his jaw. He exhaled slowly, his mouth stretching into a smile.

"It probably seems silly to an outsider," Giorgi said to me. "But the research that goes into the fiction, the writing itself, it all makes Jane and her characters more real. There was a good deal of autobiography in her stories."

"Jane Austen wrote *fiction*." Derek sneered, adjusting the collar of his navy blue suit. "Don't conflate the author with the story."

I touched my own collar. I was starting to feel underdressed in my khakis and pink floral blouse.

"Jane was marvelous," Lizzy tossed her head, and a lock of long black hair came loose from her high bun. "The author can't help but be conflated with the story, because it came from her head. Unlike AI."

Derek rolled his eyes. "Don't start on that again."

"Why not?" Lizzy slapped one hand on the table by her hip, rumpling its white cloth. "You've ruined the site with your stupid AI."

"And doubled the number of subscribers," Derek said.

"Subscribers." Kathy's upper lip curled. "Not writers, *subscribers*."

Giorgi cleared his throat. "I loved your story about Mr. Bennet and the tomato garden," he told my grandfather.

The small, dark-haired man stuck out his hand. "And I'm Martin Carlton, community liaison for—"

"Not now, Martin." Derek sighed.

Martin's face pinched. He dropped his hand and mumbled something inaudible.

Giorgi rubbed his hands together. "Where's that food?" he asked, and Martin shot him a grateful look.

"Waiting in the kitchen," I said. "I'll get it in a moment."

"Have you got any of those roast beef sandwiches?" Gramps asked me in a low voice.

"Ah, no," I said. "We're doing a regency tea with scones and recipes inspired by Jane Austen's friend and in-law, Martha Lloyd." Lloyd's personal family cookbook had been published a few years back. It was a treasure trove of insight into Jane Austen's life and the food she loved.

My grandfather's bushy white brows drew downward. "But will there be cheese toasties?"

"Oh, yeah," I said. "Those were Jane's favorites."

Gramps beamed and rubbed his hands together. "Then let's eat. I wouldn't want to have a séance on an empty stomach." He moved toward the table, and his fan-fic companions gathered around, pulling out their wooden chairs and sitting.

"You look like you swallowed arsenic," Hyperion said. "What's wrong?"

I shook myself. "Nothing. Nothing." I didn't tell my grandfather everything going on in my life. Why should he tell me about his new hobby?

My stomach quivered. *Wait. Was* it new?

Martin hurried to pull out the chair for Kathy. Without acknowledging him, she sat. He reddened and found an empty chair beside hers.

Since I'd let the waitstaff go home, I acted as waitress, bringing out individual teapots, tiered trays of scones and sandwiches, and clearing small plates. The fit around the table was as tight as I'd suspected. Gramps looked uncomfortable jammed between Derek and Kathy.

Kathy, however, appeared delighted by the seating arrangement, scooting closer to Gramps. Lizzy had given Derek a wide berth, pushing her chair away from him to do so. The man seemed popular with no one.

Beside Kathy, Martin sat a little away from the table too, as if to give the older woman more space. That didn't stop him from continually offering her scones and cheese toasties, however, or from topping up her tea every time she took a sip.

I dimmed the chandeliers, leaving only a single, tall, white candle on the table for illumination. It stood upright in what Kathy informed me was an antique chamberstock, and *not*, as I'd put it, a candle-holder-suitable-for-damsels-in-distress-on-a-haunted-staircase.

Kathy had provided it, insisting the candle provided atmosphere. She wasn't wrong. The flickering flame cast eerie, wavering shadows over the faces of the participants.

"I'm not holding hands," Derek's voice rang out.

"Ew." Hyperion made a face. "Who said anything about that? No one wants sweaty hands. Now I'd like to ask everyone to turn off your phones and—"

"Can't I just put it on silent?" Giorgi asked.

"Fine," Hyperion said, and I thought I detected a bit of tension in his voice. "Is everyone ready...? Now... relax. Visualize a protective globe of white light surrounding everyone at the table."

"Would that be a globe for each of us?" Kathy asked. "Or one surrounding the entire table?"

Hyperion sighed. "The entire table. You are protected," he intoned.

Someone snorted.

"Now close your eyes..." Hyperion continued, "and breathe deeply... Visualize a white light descending from the heavens, through the ceiling, through your head, down your spine, and into your heart... Imagine a root descending from your heart, down your spine, through the floor, and into the earth, grounding you."

I felt my way to the cool quartz of the tea bar. My hip struck a barstool, and I winced as it scraped across the laminate floor. I positioned myself behind the bar without knocking into anything else and relaxed.

Hyperion sounded like he actually knew what he was doing. *This should be interesting.*

"Visualize a golden light above the top of your head," Hyperion continued. "Breathe in... See the light expand, filling you with peace and clarity. Exhale and let any doubts and fears you may have dissolve into this loving light..."

Though I wasn't part of the séance, I caught myself imagining the light. I shifted my weight. Hyperion might be a Tarot reader rather than a medium, but his voice was oddly compelling. It was hard not to visualize along with him.

"Silently," Hyperion said, "ask anyone who wishes to communicate to do so. Let them know we are here in a spirit of peace and love..."

A chair creaked. A cold chill touched my shoulder, and I whisked my head around to look behind me. All I could make out was the dark lines of the shelves and the rows of tea canisters huddled atop them.

I rubbed the back of my neck and swallowed. *Silly.* I'd only imagined that icy touch. What ghost would drop by to see me? I wasn't even a part of the séance. But the skin on the back of my neck pebbled.

"When you're ready—" Hyperion began.

The candle blew out, and I jumped. People at the table gasped and murmured, covering the noise from my own jump scare. Blindly, I looked around. I needn't have worried about the tearoom being dark enough. I couldn't see a thing.

I rubbed my eyes, trying to adjust to the sudden darkness. The scent of flowers surrounded me, and I sneezed.

"Who's there?" Derek demanded, voice taut.

CRASH.

A woman screamed.

Reaching for the light switch beside the counter, I flipped it on. My stomach plummeted. "Oh, no."

It was a joke. It was a mistake. It was *wrong*.

It was Derek, sprawled face down on the white tablecloth.

Chapter 2

"Stop making a fool of yourself, Derek," Kathy barked. "Straighten up."

Derek remained slumped over the table. He didn't twitch, didn't groan, didn't reply.

No, no, no. I pulled my cell phone from my apron and dialed 9-1-1. In case of tearoom medical emergencies, I'd drilled to get help first and ask questions later. If Derek was playing a prank, *he* could explain it to the dispatcher. But my fingers trembled against the phone's screen.

My palms grew damp. Derek hadn't struck me as the joking type.

Giorgi rose so fast his chair tipped onto the floor with a clatter. Light from the chandeliers gleamed off his golden hair. "He's not acting." He came around the table and gripped Derek's shoulder. "What's wrong? What are you feeling?"

"Is he…?" Lurching from her chair, Lizzy pressed a hand to her mouth, catching a lock of her own dark hair. It coiled, a question mark, against her scarlet lips.

"Nine-one-one," a woman recited over the phone to me. "What is your emergency?"

"I need an ambulance," I said too fast, a lead weight filling my chest. *Get up. Tell us it's not real.* "A man's fallen unconscious." *Please, please let him be okay.*

"Where are you?" the dispatcher asked.

I gave her the address.

Kathy rose and hurried to Derek. She laid a hand on his back. "It's all right," she said quietly. "You'll be all right."

Derek choked out a groan. Giorgi patted his hands over Derek, then dropped to his knees beside him. He raised a bloodstained hand. "He's bleeding. Quick, get me a towel to stop the flow."

"Can you tell me what happened?" the dispatcher asked.

"He's bleeding from his midsection, I think," I said, tasting bile. That definitely wasn't a joke. "I... I don't know. He seems to be unconscious, or close to it." I grabbed a dish towel and hurried around the counter.

Hyperion rose and snatched it from my hand. He trotted back to the table.

"Police and an ambulance are on the way," the dispatcher told me.

Martin rose from his chair. "It will be all right," he told Kathy in a patronizing tone.

The older woman touched her throat. "I... certainly hope so."

"Press the towel to the wound," Giorgi told Hyperion. "Use pressure."

"I know." Hyperion knelt beside the man and pressed the cloth to his side. Red blossomed on the white fabric. His shoulders curled inward. "I think there's more than one puncture."

"What's that?" Gramps bent sideways in his chair as if to pick something off the laminate floor.

"Don't touch it," Giorgi said sharply.

Gramps straightened, his hands raised, showing they were empty. "It's a quill knife."

"We need more towels." Hyperion's mouth set in a grim line

I grabbed more towels from the bin beneath the counter and jogged to the table. A short-bladed knife with what looked like a bone handle lay at my grandfather's feet.

Giorgi took the towels and reached beneath Derek's slumped figure, as if to press them to the unconscious man's abdomen. He shook his head. "I can't see what I'm doing. We need to move him away from the table. Can you give me a hand?" he asked my grandfather.

Gramps hefted himself from the chair and helped him pull Derek off the table. Derek's head lolled as he leaned back against his chair.

Giorgi pressed experimentally with a towel against Derek's front and sides. "There are more punctures on this side." He glanced at Lizzy, frozen in her chair. "What the devil happened?"

"It looks like he was shanked." Gramps stepped back, his chest rising and falling. Blood stained his hands.

"What?" Lizzy asked, her face pale. "What's that?"

"Rapid stabbing with a quick upward motion into the gut," Gramps said. "If you stab someone there enough times, you're bound to hit something important."

Lizzy swayed in her chair. "I need to... I feel sick."

I pointed toward the bathroom. She raced into the hallway and vanished. A door slammed.

"Hyperion," I said in a low voice. *Please tell me he's alive.*

Hyperion met my gaze. He shook his head, and my insides bottomed. BAM BAM BAM.

I started, then jogged across the laminate floor to the blue front door. "I never locked the door," I exclaimed. It was an inane thing to say. But suddenly it seemed important that I'd left the group, the tearoom, so vulnerable in the dark.

Before I could open the door, my least favorite San Borromeo detective, Baranko, did it himself. He strode inside, the ends of his stained trench coat flapping.

"Where's the injured..." Spotting the table, the massive detective trailed off and jogged toward it. "What's the situation?

Hyperion sat back on his heels. "He's dead," he said in a dull voice. "There was too much blood."

Baranko's fleshy jaw set. The detective pressed two fingers to Derek's neck, and his nostrils flared.

"All right." Detective Baranko grasped Hyperion's shoulder. "You. Sit at that table. You." He pointed at me. "Behind the counter." He separated us all, seating the others at different tables around the tearoom.

Wiping her hands on the front of her black t-shirt, Lizzy emerged from the hallway. "What's going on?" Her heart-shaped face looked greenish.

"Where'd you come from?" Baranko asked.

"The bathroom," she said.

"You, sit over there." The detective pointed to an empty table, and she sat.

Paramedics and more police officers arrived. The paramedics confirmed what we already knew—Derek was dead.

We were questioned at different tables around the tearoom. A forensics team arrived. The séance guests were released. A policewoman rose from Hyperion's table, then my partner stood as well. Across the tearoom, Hyperion looked a question at me, and I nodded.

Gramps sat at the bar, face wan, in a pair of gray sweats. The police had confiscated his blood-stained costume as evidence.

The body was removed. Baranko left.

I felt beaten—physically and emotionally. I'd seen bodies before. There was something pitiable in a corpse—the slack expression, the ending, the inability to defend themselves from prying eyes and groping hands.

But I'd never watched someone die. I'd never watched the life drain from a person.

I never wanted to see it again.

I followed Gramps home. If I felt exhausted, he looked it, his shoulders slumped beneath his borrowed sweats.

"I'll be fine, Abigail," he said on the doorsteps of his fairytale-style house. A warm autumn breeze whispered through the ivy clinging to the white stucco turret. "It wasn't my knife, and I'm sure the police will be able to track it down."

But Gramps had been sitting beside the victim, and the police had found him covered in blood. I knew he'd gotten that blood trying to help, but they didn't.

"How can you be so sure?" I asked.

"It's a Regency-era pen knife. I've seen them in museums." A spark of color lit his rounded cheeks, and I was glad to see it. "I've always wanted one."

"Did you see or hear anything during the séance?"

He shook his head. "I was focused on the candle. When it went out, I was blind."

I studied the brick walk. "Me too." I shouldn't have let myself become entranced by the séance.

"But..." He rubbed his chin. "There was an odd sound when the candle went out. A sort of whooshing noise. Did you hear it?"

"I was pretty far away. But I'll ask Hyperion."

"I can ask him," he said.

I started to say it would be easier if I did, but I wasn't in the habit of infantilizing my grandfather. If he wanted to ask, he could ask.

But my stomach twisted into a Gordian knot. Derek had been killed right next to my grandfather. Gramps might have been a victim too. And now... he was a suspect.

Chapter 3

"It's all fun and games until someone accuses you of murder." In his office, Hyperion slumped in his thronelike chair cushioned with red velvet. He set his heels on the scarlet-clothed table.

His tabby, Bastet, stretched and yawned on the altar. The orange cat's stripey fur brushed the driftwood branch, setting the crystals dangling from it swaying. The tealights on the altar were off. Hyperion didn't like to waste the batteries.

My lipstick-pink trench coat hung from the antler coatrack in one corner. Usually, the coat's bright color cheered me. Not today.

At least it was a Monday. The tearoom was closed Mondays, and I was glad for that. Opening Beanblossom's the day after a murder seemed wrong for all sorts of reasons.

But Hyperion and I had been drawn back to the tearoom anyway. I'd come to clean... up. Now, the dining area smelled like bleach. As for why Hyperion had come...

"It's not your fault." I massaged the back of my neck.

Hyperion jerked forward in his chair, his scarf billowing off his forest-green blazer. "I know it's not my fault. I didn't kill anyone. How could it be my fault?"

Thoughtful, I studied my partner. That had been a bit of an overreaction. "You didn't organize the séance." That had been Kathy. "No one thinks we were involved."

His lean figure loosened, and he looked away, tugging at the collar of his coffee-colored turtleneck. "I know that. It's still horrible."

I didn't tell him that horrible was cleaning up bloodstains. Horrible was repositioning the tables over the spot a man had died. Horrible was the fact that a man had been murdered.

It had happened right in front of us, and we hadn't seen a damned thing.

A man was dead, and my beloved Beanblossom's had been violated. Guilt twisted my gut. This wasn't about me. A man was *dead*.

I dropped into the matching red-velvet chair opposite. I'd never admit this to Hyperion, but sometimes, after a hectic day, I'd sneak inside his office to decompress. He'd created an oasis here for clients to relax and have their cards read.

"It's Gramps I'm worried about." I rubbed my ankle with the toe of my other sneaker, rucking up the hem of my jeans. "He sat right next to the murdered man."

"I wasn't that far from Derek either, if you recall."

"What are you talking about? You were on the other side of the table."

"No, Martin was." Hyperion pulled a deck of Tarot cards from the inside pocket of his forest green blazer. He rifled through them, pulling out seven cards and arranged them in a circle around a candle in a jar.

"I sat here." He pressed a long finger against a card portraying a jester about to step off a cliff. A little white dog barked at his heels, alerting him to the danger.

I raised an eyebrow. "The Fool?"

"Let's be honest, it fits. I feel like a fool for getting suckered into that séance. What was I thinking?"

"That it would be good for business," I said heavily. I'd thought so too. And it might have been.

Hyperion pointed to the next card. "Martin's the Six of Pentacles. He's the beggar on the card. Did you see him sucking up to Kathy? Ugh." He shuddered. "Speaking of which, Kathy sat here, Queen of Pentacles."

The Queen sat in a garden. She studied a giant gold coin in her hands.

"Wait," I asked, "is she upright or reversed? I can't tell the way it's positioned around the candle."

He turned the card upside down. "Reversed. Normally, I look at reversed cards as having their energies blocked or repressed. But Kathy is materialistic and insecure, representing the negative aspects of the card."

The office was freezing. I pulled my thin, pink cardigan tighter and narrowed my eyes. "You got all that from the séance? It couldn't have lasted more than three minutes."

"I got that from the tea and scones *before* the séance. Trust me. Queen of Pentacles reversed."

Hyperion had been doing more pre-séance mingling than I had. I'd been too busy prepping scones and toasties.

Bastet dropped to the carpeted floor. The cat padded silently to a set of bookshelves.

"Kathy was next to your grandfather." He tapped the King of Cups. The King sat on the beach, waves rippling at the base of his stone throne.

"And you made him king and Kathy queen because she wants to be a couple?" Not that she had a snowball's chance. Gramps didn't put up with bullies, and he wasn't a fan of superficiality.

One corner of Hyperion's mouth lifted. "She *was* sitting practically on top of him."

"Yeah." But Gramps made a good King—a generally happy guy who knew his business.

Beside the bookshelf, the tabby stared intently at a spot on the wall.

I edged Martin's card away from the candle. "Martin was sitting a little apart from the group." To give Kathy space? Or so he could get up without being noticed to murder Derek?

"Derek sat here, the Emperor, cold and orderly and smart. And Lizzy, the Page of Cups was beside him."

I shot him a questioning look, and he shrugged. "She's an actress, creative and sensitive," he continued. "Damn, it's cold in here."

He rose and turned on a space heater disguised as a wood stove. It hummed to life. Wavering, orange lights flowed across the fake logs, simulating fire.

"And Giorgi is the Hanged Man?" I asked.

My partner returned to his high-backed chair and dropped into it heavily. "He's in a holding pattern, waiting to sell off that Jane Austen letter and make his fortune. What did your grandfather tell you?"

"Not much."

Hyperion goggled at me. "The key witness is your grandfather, and all you got out of him was *not much*?"

I sucked in my cheeks. "He was exhausted. I didn't want to drag the night out any further. He did say he heard a whooshing noise before the candle went out."

Bastet turned his head toward us. The tabby howled, a mournful sound, and I shivered.

Hyperion frowned. "Hold on. I think I heard a whoosh too." He shook his head.

"Can you get a little more specific?"

He rubbed his knuckles over his bottom lip. "There was a *whoosh*. The candle flame went out. People mumbling and gasping. I couldn't see a damn thing for at least a minute. I'd been staring at that stupid candle the whole time. I never should have used that fire hazard. The ones in here are battery-powered." He motioned toward the tealights on the altar.

"The candle was very atmospheric." *Atmospheric and deadly.*

Hyperion met my gaze. "This murder was planned."

Yes. It had to have been. It was too perfect.

Heat raced to the front of my skull, and I flattened my mouth. We'd been used, Hyperion and I, to commit murder. Derek wasn't dead because of us, but we'd been unwitting accomplices.

So had my grandfather. My jaw set. "I think it's time you and Gramps exchanged notes."

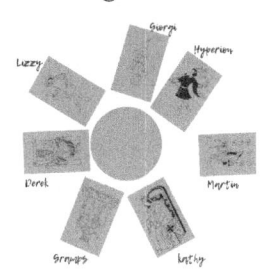

"Whoosh, crash, scream." In his kitchen, Gramps rubbed the back of his head, ruffling his wispy white hair. "I knew the crash was Derek falling on the table, since I was right next to him. Who screamed?"

Hyperion braced his elbows on my grandfather's white tile counter and shrugged. "One of the women, obviously."

Gramps cocked his head. "Obviously?"

"It wasn't *me*," my partner said testily.

A branch scraped against the house, and I glanced out the sliding glass door. A gust of wind shook the silhouettes of oak branches outside.

Gramps frowned. "Is that the same scarf you were wearing last night?" My grandfather's mallard, Peking, quacked up at him from the laminate floor.

Hyperion ran his hands down the ends of the emerald scarf. "It's Versace," he said smugly. "It goes with *everything*."

"You must be doing well." My grandfather shot me a sidelong look. "Isn't that expensive?"

"Uh, I got a deal on it," Hyperion admitted.

Gramps snapped his fingers. "Hold on. Wasn't that fellow murdered?"

"Yes," I said slowly. "Derek was murdered." Had my grandfather forgotten? Oh, no. My breath thinned, my stomach rolling. Was he starting to—?

"Not Derek," Gramps said. "Versace."

Hyperion clutched his scarf. "That's not why I got it!"

"No, no," Gramps said, pacifying. "I'm sure the scarf's not haunted or anything. It's just a coincidence that you wore it to a murder."

Hyperion flushed. "I didn't wear it *to* a murder. I was just wearing it."

"Tell Hyperion about the quill knife," I said to my grandfather before he could dig in any deeper.

"It's a knife used to sharpen quill pens," he said. "That's what Derek was killed with. Jane Austen probably used one."

I rubbed my chin. "The blade was pretty short for a murder."

"Not for a shanking," Hyperion said, and I stared. "What?" My partner shrugged. "Your grandfather was right. My martial arts instructor wrote a paper on them. He went into the prisons to learn how shankings were done and to develop defenses against them." He shot his hands forward, crossing them at the wrist to block an imaginary attack.

"I can know random facts too," Hyperion continued. "And the 1997 murder of a fashion designer by a serial killer in Miami Beach has *nothing* to do with Derek's death." He splayed one hand across his chest.

"Of course not," my grandfather said, tucking his chin.

Moving on. "How well do you know the others in the group?" I asked my grandfather.

He rolled a blueberry across the linoleum floor. The duck snatched it up before it could roll beneath the nickel oven. "Not well at all. We'd talked online, but it was all Jane Austen. Giorgi's letter was the biggest news in the group. That and Derek's appearance at the séance."

"What do you mean?" I asked.

"He's not a member of our writing group," Gramps said. "He owns—owned—the site that hosts our fan-fic and discussions. Technically, he's the managing partner. We were surprised when Kathy told us he was coming."

"Why did he come?" I asked.

"Kathy said he wanted to get feedback on the website," he said. "Apparently, he's a hands-on sort of guy."

"And Giorgi's letter was big news?" I asked. "Because Giorgi made it sound like he had the letter before he'd joined the group."

"Yeah," Gramps said, "but he didn't tell us right away. Oh, he hinted he had something big. I thought he was full of it, and I don't like hinting, so I didn't probe. But he said he was waiting to get the letter authenticated before saying anything—didn't want to be made a fool of. I can understand that."

"And Kathy wanted to buy the letter?" I asked.

"Kathy and Derek," Gramps said. "They were sort of competing with each other."

"Online?" I asked. "I mean, were they chatting about it on your fan-fic site?"

Gramps nodded.

"Can I see those web chats or texts or whatever they were?" I said.

"Sure." Gramps pulled a laptop toward him on the counter and booted it up. "It's all right..." His round face scrunched. "Hold up. It's gone."

"What do you mean, gone?" Hyperion asked.

Gramps swiveled the laptop on the counter to face him. "There's nothing there. The chat is empty."

Hyperion studied the laptop. He tapped the keyboard and frowned. "I'm on a Tarot chat like this. It looks like everything's been deleted. Who's the group administrator?"

"Martin," Gramps said.

"We'll have a talk with him later," Hyperion said.

Gramps rolled another blueberry to the mallard. "Good. I have some notes for his latest chapter that I never typed up. I want to give them to him personally." He gave me a significant look over his glasses. "I suspect it was written by AI, though he claims otherwise."

I cleared my throat. "Oh, we can take those to him for you." I didn't want to drag my grandfather into a murder investigation.

My grandfather straightened. "That murder happened right next to me. I'm the prime suspect. I'm talking to Martin too." He plucked his cabbie-style hat off the counter. "Let's see Lizzy first though."

"Ah... what?" I asked.

"She sat on Derek's other side." My grandfather fitted the cap to his head. A tuft of white hair stuck out above one ear. "Since I didn't kill him, she's the next logical choice. She's got rehearsals at the Ostrich Farm Theater today."

Hyperion squinted at him. "And you know this because... you have *not* been stalking her?"

"She invited our group down to watch the rehearsal last week," Gramps said.

My forehead wrinkled. Gramps was involved in this, no question. But I didn't like the idea of dragging him in any deeper. The last time I'd let a suspect go on an investigation, it hadn't gone well for her.

Hyperion and I had done this before. Derek had been killed in Beanblossom's, so we were obviously going to stick our noses in. But my grandfather... "Are you sure you want to—?"

"I'm going," Gramps said.

I looked to Hyperion for backup.

Hyperion straightened off the counter. "Absolutely you're going. This is your show."

I hung my head. Gramps was going.

Chapter 4

I DIDN'T BOTHER ASKING Hyperion if he thought bringing Gramps was a good idea—*bad* ideas enthralled him. And I didn't need to protect my grandfather from the actress. Gramps would be insulted by the idea.

I grouched in the backseat of my grandfather's Lincoln instead.

We bumped over the dirt road to the theater. An ostrich fluffed its gray wings and peered through the wire fence at my Grandfather's Lincoln.

Gramps parked in a dirt parking lot beside a red barn. The three of us stepped from the sedan.

Straightening the lapels of his green blazer, Hyperion wandered to the wire fence, his silk scarf dancing in the wind. A trio of ostriches started toward the fence.

"They might think you have food," I warned.

"I wonder what ostriches eat?" My partner dug in the pocket of his blazer and pulled out half a napkin-wrapped scone. He crumbled it and tossed it through the fence. The ostriches trotted closer.

"Don't give them my scones," I snapped.

"Right," Hyperion said, contrite, "they might not be healthy for them."

I'd been offended by the waste of a good scone. But I didn't mention that.

"That's not why I wouldn't feed them," Gramps said. "Ostriches are biters."

An ostrich strolled in front of the barn doors, sat, and fluffed his white tipped wings. Cocking his head, the bird studied us.

I edged closer to his Lincoln. "Biters?" Even seated on the ground, it was an awfully big bird.

"Relax." Hyperion turned from the fence. "They wouldn't let it roam around if it was dangerous. This is California, land of lawsuits and liability."

The bird guarding the barn snorted. I stopped short.

"Come on." Hyperion ambled toward the barn door. "We've got to go in sometime."

Flapping its wings, the ostrich rose to its feet. The bird towered over Hyperion. My partner hesitated.

"Nope. Biters." Gramps got inside his Lincoln. "Come on, Abigail." He shut the door.

Leaving the door open, I slithered into the car's back seat behind him. "Maybe we can just call Lizzy from the car?"

"Yeah..." Hyperion said and edged toward the Lincoln. The ostrich took a step closer and made a low, hooting sound.

"I don't have her number." Gramps pulled his phone from the pocket of his brown, plaid jacket. "I can send Lizzy an email though." He adjusted his glasses and squinted at the phone. "Damn buttons are too small."

The ostrich snapped at Hyperion, and he yelped and jerked away. The scarf flew upward. Hyperion whipped around, his scarf pulling free. My partner raced toward the car. The ostrich tossed his head, and one end of the scarf arced upward.

Hyperion wrenched open the driver's side door and launched himself into the Lincoln. He panted. "Or we can wait."

The ostrich circled the sedan. The scarf trailed from his beak.

Hyperion's brown eyes widened. "Hey!" He rolled down his window. "That's mine. It's Versace!"

"How *did* you get your hands on a Versace?" I asked conversationally. I suspected we were in for a long wait before Lizzy rescued us.

"I found it in a Goodwill store last weekend," Hyperion admitted. "Can you believe it? They had it marked for fifteen bucks. Give me back that scarf!" He shook his fist at the ostrich.

The bird made another triumphal circuit around the car then darted down the driveway. It vanished behind the red barn.

"Versace in a Goodwill store?" I asked.

"O.M.G.," Hyperion sagged against the soft leather seat. "Priorities! That bird stole my scarf."

"Possession is nine-tenths of the law," Gramps said.

Hyperion sighed. "It's their Palo Alto store, where all the nouveau riche donate the stuff they've used twice and gotten bored with. You really should check it out," he added.

The bird trotted behind the wire fence, scarf fluttering in its beak. He raced toward a line of eucalyptus trees.

"My scarf," Hyperion said, plaintive.

Gramps patted his shoulder. "I hate to lose a good deal too."

The barn's red door opened, and Lizzy stepped out in a black t-shirt and jeans. Her t-shirt read: *Acting is my Cardio*. She waved at the Lincoln. "Come on in."

We stepped from the sedan. Scanning for ostriches, I followed Hyperion and my grandfather to the barn.

"There's an ostrich on the loose," Gramps told her. "You need to be careful."

"Did Oscar get out again?" She shook her head, her long brown curls bouncing. "Darn it. I'll phone the owner. Come on in."

"He stole my scarf." Hyperion folded his arms. "It's Versace."

We followed her inside a barn lined with metal folding chairs. My grandfather removed his cap and looked around.

A stage draped in black curtains stood at the opposite end. The set on it seemed to portray a Regency-era drawing room. Below and to the right of the stage, a handful of people chatted around an upright piano.

While Lizzy called the theater's owner, Hyperion made his way to the stage. He struck a pose. "To be, or not to be," he thundered, "that is all I remember."

I blew out my breath. We were here about a murder, not to joke around onstage. But at least he wasn't going on about his scarf anymore.

Lizzy strode toward us through the rows of chairs. She jammed her phone in the rear pocket of her jeans. "The owner will take care of the bird."

"And my scarf?" Hyperion pressed a hand to his forest-green blazer.

"He'll try." She rolled her neck. "Want to go on stage?"

"We'd love to," my grandfather said, and we followed her up a short set of steps to the stage.

Lizzy dropped into an ornate armchair. Her gaze darted around the set. "I'd hoped this would be fun for everyone. I mean... *Sense and Sensibility.* It's Austen. But now..." She looked toward a painted fireplace and bit her bottom lip.

Gramps perched on the nearby settee. "How are you holding up? It was quite a shock last night, even if we only knew each other online."

Lizzy swallowed. "I'm trying to not think about it by working."

"I suppose this theater is too small for private dressing rooms," Hyperion said.

"Oh, no." Lizzy rose from the chair. "I mean, we don't have private dressing rooms, but there's a men's and women's dressing room. Want to see them? No one's changing now."

"I'd like to," I said.

"It's this way." Lizzy walked off stage, and we followed her past black curtains and into a narrow corridor. She opened a door with a triangle woman painted on the front, and I followed her inside.

Gramps and Hyperion hesitated in the hallway.

"It's all right," she said. "You can come in. It's just us, and like I said, no one's changing. The matinee performance isn't for three more hours."

The two men glanced at each other, then walked inside the dressing room. A long wooden counter covered in makeup kits and toiletries lined one wall. An equally long row of stick-on mirrors lined the wall behind it. Racks of costumes jammed in the corners of the narrow room.

Lizzy plucked a feathered hat from a hat stand and put it on her head. "And this is where the transformation happens." Her voice cracked.

Hyperion shot me a look. Lizzy was trying to play it casual, but she'd obviously been hit hard by what had happened. Murder had flattened us all.

My Grandfather walked to the costume racks and peered at the gowns. "These are more detailed than I'd have expected for the stage."

"One of our actresses is a cos-player. She made a lot of these costumes." She returned the hat to its stand and drew her fingers through the feathers.

"Atlanta?" Gramps asked. "She's the one who lent me my costume the other night. I hated breaking it to her about the bloodstains, but she was pretty even-keeled about it. And about the police confiscating it."

"Did Derek ever see you perform?" I asked her.

Lizzy's hand jerked, knocking the feathered hat from its stand and to the wood board floor. Swiftly, she bent and picked it up. "I don't think so. I mean, not lately."

My grandfather's broad forehead wrinkled. "You mean, you knew him? Offline?"

Her gaze shifted. "We... dated, briefly."

She'd dated the murdered man? My opinion of Lizzy's acting skills rose. If I'd watched someone I'd dated die, even if we'd only dated briefly, I'd be a wreck. She was hiding her distress well.

"I didn't know," I said. "I'm sorry."

"Don't be." Her gaze met mine in the mirror. "It wasn't for very long."

"How awful for you though," I said.

"Yes. I don't know who..." Lizzy trailed off.

"Would have wanted to kill him?" I asked in a low tone.

"The police seemed to think I might have." She laughed shakily. "Just because I was sitting next to Derek when... when..." She burst into tears.

My grandfather came to pat her shoulder. "No one thinks you did it."

Didn't we? Lizzy was obviously stressed, and though that could have been from being next to a man when he was killed... Okay, that *was* the most likely explanation. But still, she'd been right next to Derek when he was stabbed.

Lizzy sniffed. "Excuse me." She strode from the dressing room.

"We should leave," my grandfather said.

"An emotional breakdown is exactly the time we should stay," Hyperion said.

Gramps frowned. "I know she's a suspect, but I didn't come here to make the poor girl cry."

"Ah..." I winced. "Hyperion's right. People reveal more when they're under pressure, even if what they're revealing is untruthful." Amateur detecting could be a dirty business.

"I know that," my grandfather said. "I just don't like it."

"Forget about it," a woman's voice rose in the hallway.

I edged toward the door and peeked out.

A young woman in jeans and a t-shirt stood with her hands on her hips in front of Lizzy. "I'm not giving you any more money. A, I don't have any. And B, you haven't paid me back from the last time."

Lizzy responded in a voice too low for me to hear. Ears straining, I leaned farther into the hallway.

The woman snorted and brushed past her. "Ask your dumb dandy."

Hastily, I ducked back into the dressing room, and my elbow bumped a rack of costumes. They swayed, phantomlike. *Huh.* Lizzy needed money. But did it mean anything?

Hyperion pantomimed a *"well?"*

I rubbed my elbow and mouthed, *"Later."*

Lizzy returned. "I'm sorry. Meeting here was a bad idea so soon after what happened."

"Did you see or hear anything last night that might indicate what *did* happen?" I asked.

She shook her head. A lock of carob-colored hair loosed from her bun and coiled against her slender neck. "I thought... I thought I sensed someone walk behind me. But then Derek fell forward, and I screamed like a little girl. After that, I was focused on him."

Hyperion shot me an I-told-you-it-wasn't-me look. I shrugged. One question, answered.

"Did you see or hear him fall forward?" I asked her.

"Heard, mostly," Lizzy said. "When that candle went out, I couldn't see anything for a minute or two."

"Did Derek have any enemies in the group?" I asked.

Her laugh was scalpel sharp. "Enemies?"

"Had he argued with anyone?" I amended.

"He was constantly baiting Kathy," Lizzy said slowly.

"About what?" Hyperion asked.

"Her role as group leader, that stupid letter of Giorgi's—"

"Stupid?" my grandfather asked.

Lizzy grimaced. "A letter by Jane Austen and about writing of all things is amazing. But the way Derek and Kathy were battling over it... Giorgi loved the rivalry, of course, after—" She snapped her mouth shut.

I cocked my head. "After wha—?"

BANG.

Lizzy shrieked and jumped. She pressed a hand to her heart. The hat stand lay on its side, rocking slowly on the rough wood floor. Shattered glass from a broken mason jar sparkled around its base.

She bent to pick up what was left of the jar. "How clumsy of me," she said, not meeting my gaze.

"You were saying?" I prompted. "After..."

"After Derek and Kathy were bidding up the price," she said.

"If you know or suspect anything," my grandfather said, "it's dangerous to keep it back."

"I'm not," she said hotly. "Do you think—? I'm not involved. I would never kill anyone."

"I know," Gramps said. "But sometimes we tell ourselves that the truth won't help, or that it will hurt. The fact is, it's the lies that do more damage—to ourselves and others."

"I don't know what you're talking about," she said coldly.

Gramps sighed and took my arm. "Let's go, Abigail." To Lizzy, he said, "Thank you for showing us the set."

"He's right," Hyperion said. "If you can think of anything that might help, let us know."

"Let the *police* know." Gramps said.

"Right." Hyperion nodded. "The police."

Grimacing, Gramps steered Hyperion and I outside. A gust of wind slammed the barn door behind us.

I was pretty sure Lizzy had knocked that hat stand sideways intentionally. And I was pretty sure she didn't care about the bidding war. Uneasy, I bit the inside of my cheek. What was she hiding?

Chapter 5

"AM I THE ONLY one who thinks ostriches don't make the best pets?" I asked.

"Don't ask me," Gramps said. "I have a duck."

The Lincoln bumped past the theater's wire fence. Behind it, a man played tug of war with an ostrich. Hyperion's scarf dangled from the other side of its beak.

Hyperion propped his elbow on the car's open window. Head on his fist, he whispered, "Versace."

"*Gesundheit*," Gramps said. "What exactly did that other actress say to Lizzy?"

"She said Lizzy should ask her dumb dandy," I replied.

One-handed, Gramps adjusted his cabby hat. "Hm. A dandy's a man who's particularly fashionable. Know anyone like that?"

"Giorgi," Hyperion said flatly. "Did you see? He's not the brightest bulb, and he was wearing a Zegna linen shirt last night."

The car jounced over a rut. We swayed in our seats.

"What's a Zegna?" Gramps turned the car onto the highway.

"Expensive," Hyperion said.

"How expensive?" I asked.

"Over $800 for a shirt expensive."

Gramps whistled. "What kind of person wastes that kind of money on a shirt?"

I sympathized. When he'd been a CPA, he'd had some seriously wealthy clients. None of them got that way buying $800 shirts. And after they'd made it, they still didn't blow money on clothes.

"She *could* be dating some other dumb dandy," I said.

We zipped past lush green fields dotted with pumpkins. Halloween was on its way.

"Ye-es," Hyperion said, "but I definitely caught a vibe between her and Giorgi. And we need to talk to him anyway."

"I'd really like to see that letter," Gramps said wistfully. "But I have to get back home. Peking has a vet appointment today."

"Is something wrong with him?" I leaned forward in the back seat. I liked the mallard.

"No. It's time for his checkup."

"We'll all track down Giorgi tomorrow," Hyperion said. "Abs and I can do online research today."

Gramps chuckled. "Don't you mean your friend Razzzor can do it for you?"

Hyperion sniffed. "I am perfectly capable of conducting a web search."

Razzzor was my ex-boss, current online gaming partner, and all-around tech genius. He'd created his latest company mainly because he'd been bored. It had taken off. All of Razzzor's projects did. He was weirdly charmed.

Or maybe it wasn't so weird. I suspected he succeeded because he was passionate about his projects.

We dropped Gramps off at his house, and Hyperion and I returned to my bungalow. I rented it from my grandfather's best friend, and I loved it—and not only because of the cheap rent.

The exterior was sunshine yellow. It had a surprisingly long backyard, where I'd built raised beds for my herbs and vegetables. The redwood deck was perfect for warm evenings.

Inside, its bamboo floors and white-brick fireplace gave it a cozy feel. Hyperion dropped onto my blue sofa and motioned toward the gaming controllers and headset lying on the cushions. "We're alone. Summon Razzzor."

I folded my arms and leaned against the door frame. "No."

He frowned. "Why not? He can find out anything about anyone if it's online."

"And Razzzor's got a business to run. We can't call him whenever we want and demand dark-web snooping." I was starting to feel guilty about it.

"How are *we* supposed to do it?"

I opened up the laptop on my dining room table. "The old-fashioned way. Web searches and social media."

Lizzy, being an actress, was all over social media. While Hyperion scrolled through his phone, I bookmarked her videos to watch later.

"Ha!" Hyperion shouted.

I looked up from my laptop. "*Ha*, what?"

"Lizzy and Giorgi. I *knew* they were an item." He brandished his phone.

Rising, from my chair. I walked to the couch to squint. On Hyperion's screen, Lizzy kissed Giorgi's cheek, her lips puckered exaggeratedly.

"Are there photos of her with any other members of the fan fic group?" I asked.

"Um..." He scrolled down. "No. What about you?"

I returned to my laptop and sat. "I found some articles about Derek's literary tech startup. Giorgi's name is mentioned as a partner in the earlier articles, but then it's all just Derek."

Hyperion came to stand behind me. "Tech startup, hm? Now who would know something about tech startups?" He snapped his fingers. "I've got it. Maybe... *Razzzor* can help us."

I scowled. "Leave Razzzor out of this." I typed in the name of the startup, and the browser took me to a website in subdued grays called *TalesTrove*.

"TalesTrove looks like an interactive story platform," Hyperion said. "Look. People can write and read fan fiction and vote on the story's direction."

"And there are discussion boards." I clicked the button. It took me to a page asking for $9.99 a month to participate.

Nine-ninety-nine a month? Gramps didn't even pay for cable. He said TV rotted the brain, but really it was because he was cheap. As a small business owner, this was a quality I'd come to respect. I knew he missed the History channel though.

What was going *on* with Gramps? I brushed back my hair with one hand.

"Anything on Kathy?" Hyperion asked.

I opened a web tab. "Yeah. She's all over the society pages—or what passes for them nowadays." Kathy was apparently a prime mover and shaker in the local non-profit scene. If there was a gala or fundraiser, her name was mentioned.

"Martin has an Instagram page," he said.

"Who? Oh, right." I was ashamed to admit I'd kind of forgotten about the little man who'd been bowing and scraping over Kathy at the séance. "Anything good there?"

"Lots of food porn, but the lighting's terrible." He showed me his phone screen. The page was filled with photos of Martin's meals. The lighting *was* terrible.

"Archer might know something. He covers society gossip." Archer was a friend of my grandfather's. He'd recently made the switch from newspapers to the online world. He claimed he hated it, but he was devastatingly good at what he did.

"If we call Archer, *we'll* end up in the gossip pages. Can we call Razzzor now?" Hyperion asked pointedly. "Because I'm not impressed with our progress."

Neither was I. "Fine." I picked up my gaming headset and logged onto Razzzor's game, *Zombie Nazis in Space*. It took about five minutes of blasting zombie Nazis across a desert planet before Razzzor joined me.

"Watch your six," he bellowed.

PEW, PEW, PEW!

I winced. Turning down the volume on my headset, I repositioned my avatar.

Razzzor's avatar, in full body armor, leapt over a boulder and blasted a final zombie. "Hey, Abs. Haven't seen you around for a while. I heard about the séance. Bad luck about the murder." The planets red rocks reflected, warped, in his visor.

"Yeah." I shifted on the soft cushions. "I don't suppose you could, er, get some background on the people who were there that night?"

Beside me on the couch, Hyperion looked up from his phone.

Razzzor dropped his arm, his laser blaster hanging limp at his side. "Uh, that's the thing..."

"What?" I asked, surprised. Razzzor was usually eager to use his skills in the cause of Lady Justice.

"I've got a new HR manager, and she's, uh..."

I made a face. "Young and attractive?" My ex-boss was also the target of every available gold digger in Silicon Valley. Plenty of unavailable ones were hot on his trail too.

"No. I mean, well, yes, she is, but—"

"Razzzor..."

"It's not that," he said crossly. "She's pointed out—correctly—that it's unethical for me to use our firm's background check company for personal reasons."

"What?" Hyperion asked. "What's he saying?"

I covered the speaker with my hand. "He's saying HR's giving him grief."

"Doesn't he *pay* HR?" Hyperion arched a brow.

"Is that Hyperion?" Razzzor asked.

"Yeah." I switched the sound to the speakers bracketing my TV on the mantel and yanked off my headset. "Hyperion was running the séance. And you're on speaker."

"I didn't think Hyperion was a medium."

"I'm not," Hyperion said. "I'm a séance resources expert."

"Ha, ha," my ex-boss said in a dry tone.

"Look," I said, "if you can't use your background check thing, do you know anything about an online literary company started up by Derek Benson?"

"I guess I could ask," Razzzor said doubtfully.

"Thanks," I said.

Razzzor blasted an orangeish bit of rock to smithereens. "Fine. What are the names of those people you wanted me to check on?"

I recited the list of suspects.

"Okay... Hold on..."

Elevator music played over the speakers, and I frowned. When had he added *that* as a game feature? And when had eighties tunes become elevator music? That was just wrong.

"Is Razzzor being more weird than usual?" Hyperion asked. "When did he start caring about business ethics?"

"Always," I whispered. "He just doesn't care about *rules*."

"Why are you whispering?" he asked.

"Because I'm on hold. It just seems polite."

Hyperion raised a brow. "You're worried about being polite to Razzzor?"

"There are currant scones in the kitchen," I said.

"I don't want a currant scone."

"I do."

"Fine." He huffed and rose. "I'll get you one. I suppose you want lemon curd, too."

"Yes, please."

I'd finished half my scone when Razzzor returned to the line. Hyperion had thoughtfully warmed it in the microwave. It was flaky and delicious—like a biscuit but sweeter. The lemon curd was the perfect accompaniment.

"Okay," Razzzor said, "none of your suspects have criminal histories."

"And?" A clot of lemon curd dropped onto my jeans. I brushed it off with a napkin.

"That's it," Razzzor said. "Seriously, I can't do more than that with our current service without raising red flags."

"Since when did you care about red flags?" I straightened on the couch. "It's your company."

"You haven't met HR," he said dismally and disconnected.

"Well?" Hyperion asked between bites of the scone he hadn't wanted. Crumbs dribbled onto the blue sofa.

"None of our suspects have criminal pasts."

"And?"

"That's what I said. That was all the info Razzzor could give us. But he said he'd nose around about that fan-fic company."

Hyperion finished the scone and swallowed. "So. We're on our own."

"Yeah." My lips tightened. Not that Razzzor had been the backbone of our investigations in the past. We'd been on our own before. But now we were on our own and my grandfather was the stakes.

I didn't like it one bit.

Chapter 6

Behind me, my cell phone rang on the dining room table. I jumped off the couch and hurried to check the screen. *My grandfather*. Anxiety swamped my usual pleasure. Was Peking okay? Had Gramps gone investigating on his own?

I answered. "Hi, Gramps."

"Want to see the letter this afternoon?" my grandfather asked.

I stepped away from the table and edged a blue curtain aside. Behind the French doors, my garden was bursting with summer's end enthusiasm.

Releasing the curtain, I shot Hyperion a glance. My partner tapped away at his phone. I suspected he was texting his boyfriend rather than searching for online clues.

"I thought you had to take Peking to the vet?" I hedged.

"I did. We're back. We can go see the Austen letter now. I've arranged it with Giorgi."

"Put him on speaker," Hyperion said.

Grimacing, I did.

"What have you got?" Hyperion asked.

"A meeting with Giorgi for this afternoon," my grandfather said. "You in?"

"For another madcap adventure?" my partner asked. "If it's ostrich-free, I'm there. Should we pick you up?"

"Nope," Gramps said. "I'm outside."

"Toot toot. Let's bounce." Putting words to action, Hyperion bounced off my couch.

I disconnected. With a sigh, I plucked my pink trench coat from the back of my dining room chair.

"What's the problem?" my partner asked.

"Don't you think this is a little... weird? Using my grandfather to get to suspects?"

Hyperion shrugged into his green blazer. "Using *him*? He's using *us*."

"I just don't think this is a good idea."

"Don't tell me you're still miffed about him having a secret life?"

My brows drew downward. "Of course not. He can do what he wants."

"Good, because I think investigating with your grandfather is fun and charming. And he's waiting." He strode to my front door and stepped onto the faded redwood landing.

We drove in my grandfather's Lincoln to a condo overlooking the beach. Gramps had to circle the block twice before he found a parking spot.

Hyperion stepped from the car and stretched. "Pretty swank address. Where did you say Giorgi got his money from?"

"I didn't," Gramps said, "because I have no idea."

He pressed an intercom button in the alcove on the street.

"Yes?" Giorgi's voice crackled over the speaker.

"It's Frank Beanblossom. I'm here with Abigail and Hyperion."

The intercom buzzed, and a lock clicked open in the glass door. My grandfather opened it, and we strolled inside.

We rode the elevator to the second floor. The hallway's thick carpet muted our footsteps as we walked past oil paintings of the coast.

A door opened a few feet ahead of us, and Giorgi stepped out. "Come on in." He made an after-you motion with both arms.

I blinked. He wore a navy letterman vest under a burgundy and blue pinstriped jacket and matching slacks. The outfit was blinding.

Hyperion sucked in his breath. "Is that Todd Snyder?"

"Good eye," Giorgi said. "I like bold colors, especially since the coast is moving into foggy season."

We followed him into an artfully decorated studio. Persian rugs decorated the floors, and African masks hung from the walls. Above the gas fireplace hung a pair of crossed spears.

"From Tanzania," he said, catching me studying them. "Don't worry, the blades are dull."

I shuddered. Someone had thrown a javelin at me once. It had missed and had been an accident. *Mostly*...

"From your travels?" Gramps asked.

"There's something about Africa," Giorgi enthused. "It's so diverse, it's a bit foolish to say one traveled to Africa. Which part? The mountains of Ethiopia? The red dunes of the Zambian coast? The Egyptian pyramids or a safari in the Sahara?"

The speech sounded practiced. But Giorgi's enthusiasm was contagious. I wanted to see the red dunes of Zambia.

"Do you travel for work?" Hyperion asked.

"For pleasure, mainly. Would you like something to drink? Brandy? Tequila? I have Patron."

Hyperion, a tequila snob, perked up. "Which kind?"

"El Alto."

"I'll have a glass," my partner said.

"Frank? Abigail?"

We murmured our no thank you's. Giorgi walked to the open kitchen, its quartz countertops shimmering like mercury. On the counter, a thick candle stood in a wooden holder decorated with lions.

"I suppose you're wondering how I came across the Jane Austen letter," he said from behind the counter.

"You said it was a family heirloom?" my grandfather asked.

"Not exactly." Giorgi uncorked a blue bottle with a soft pop. "It did come through my family, but I don't think anyone realized what they had. The letter was in an old trunk, from an elderly aunt on my mother's side. I suspect the only reason no one threw it away was because they were too lazy." He grinned and poured out two shot glasses. "I come from a long line of people who've beaten workaholism. I'm decades sober myself."

"Not too lazy to go through that old trunk," I said.

Giorgi's brow creased. "No, I suppose I got curious. My father was a rare book restorer, you know. I hoped to find first editions inside." He shook himself. "I'm sorry he never got to see the Austen letter. He would have recognized it instantly." He walked around the counter and handed Hyperion a glass. "Skoll."

They clinked glasses, and Giorgi knocked back his drink. Hyperion sipped the tequila, his expression thoughtful.

"But you want to see the letter." Giorgi sat the glass on the counter. "Just one moment, I'll get it." He walked into another room.

I examined a small African figurine on the mantel. A piece of blue peeked from beneath it, and I carefully lifted the figurine. A sticker from World Market was stuck to its base.

Walking to the counter, I checked beneath the candlestick. *Made in China.*

I shook my head. *So much for travels to the African continent.* It was a sad state of affairs if Giorgi thought he had to impress *us*.

"Here we go," Giorgi called.

Hastily, I returned the candlestick, knocking aside the matchsticks littered about its base.

Giorgi set a beige cardboard box on the glass dining table. He lifted the lid, exposing a letter atop a rectangle of foam padding. "I'll have to ask you not to touch it. Oils on your fingers, you know."

My grandfather extracted a pair of reading glasses from the inside pocket of his brown jacket. Setting it on his nose, he bent, studying the letter. "*My Dear Susan?* Do you know who Susan was?"

"Indeed," Giorgi said. "Susan Grimshaw was one of my ancestors. She grew up in Steventon."

"Where Jane lived before moving with her family to Bath," Gramps said excitedly.

Giorgi nodded toward the box. "From Jane's letter, it appears young Susan had pretensions to be a poet. Alas, if she was, none of her work survived."

Gramps squinted at the letter. "Jane was encouraging though. She was a kind woman."

"When she wanted to be." One corner of Giorgi's mouth tilted upward. My grandfather pored over the letter.

"You say your father was a book restorer?" I asked, and Giorgi nodded. "Was that why you got involved in developing the fan fic website? A love of books?"

He stiffened. "I was only briefly involved in TalesTrove's creation."

"What happened?" Hyperion set his empty shot glass on the table.

"It turned out web development was *not* one of my areas of expertise." His handsome face flushed. "And… if you must know, I got bounced out. Not because of lack of skill or effort. But Derek saw it was going to be a success, and the greedy bastard wanted it all." He smiled briefly. "So there. I had a motive to kill him. Is that what you wanted to know?"

"I didn't know you were involved in the website." My grandfather straightened away from the dining table. His expression was regretful.

"Derek made sure to erase all trace of my contribution. I'm surprised you knew about it."

I shrugged. "The tech world is a small one, at least in Silicon Valley."

Giorgi motioned toward the letter in its gray cardboard box. "I was hoping to make up for the loss with this."

"You still can, can't you?" I asked. "If Kathy buys it?"

"I hope so."

"How much is it worth?" Hyperion asked.

"This?" Giorgi angled his head. "The last letter of Jane's that was up for auction went for nearly two hundred grand. It's valuable, but not worth killing over, if that's what you're thinking"

Not for the money, no. But for a piece of Jane? A piece of literary history? My stomach hardened. *Maybe.*

Chapter 7

As much as I loved spending time with my grandfather, it was a relief to deposit him at his house. It was also a relief to get back to work the next day.

I confess, I'd been worried a murder in Beanblossom's might frighten off customers. True, profit and loss was nothing compared to murder. But I had staff to pay. Beanblossom's success might not matter as much as murder, but it mattered.

I needn't have worried. Tuesday afternoon was busy.

Suspiciously busy.

"Tell me *everything*." Archer, tearoom regular and online gossip columnist braced his elbow on the table. The silver-haired man looked like he'd just stepped off a yacht in his double-breasted blue blazer, ascot, and white shirt and slacks. "I heard that battle axe Kathy Landsford was there."

Battle axe? I wiped down the white counter. I'd been hoping he'd stop by, but now I wasn't sure how to approach this. "Ah, I'm not sure I can say much. It's a police investigation."

Tarot readers moved between tables. Women and a few men drank tea and snapped photos. Occasionally, people snapped pictures of their tea tiers for Instagram. Today, I suspected they wanted shots of the murder scene.

"Were you really trying to summon the ghost of Jane Eyre?" Archer asked. "She's fictional, you know."

"Jane Austen." I topped up his teacup with more oolong. "And I wasn't doing the summoning, Hyperion was."

"I didn't think he was a medium. What a talented young man." He shivered. "Murder at a séance, the killer moving through the dark on silent feet..." The older man made a face. "No, it's too much. How the hell did the killer pull it off?"

"If I knew that, I'd tell the police," I said grumpily. I was starting to understand what people felt like when I interrogated *them*.

"What did you see? You were there, weren't you?"

As if I'd miss an opportunity for a séance. "I was at the counter serving, not participating."

"And you didn't see *anything*?"

I wiped my damp hands on my sunflower apron. Hyperion had given it to me last year as part of an apron-of-the-month club. "Not much. While the candle was lit, I could make out people's faces. Barely. But when it went out—"

Archer leaned forward. A splotch of tea darkened his ascot. "The candle went out? How? Why?"

"I don't know." I rubbed my watch. It had to be near 1:30, when we would start our second seating. I had a strong suspicion the gossip columnist wasn't going to leave until he'd milked me for everything I could remember.

"I suppose everyone thought the author's ghost had arrived. And now you have a *real* ghost," he said gaily. "Of course, it was the killer who blew out the candle. Really, Abigail. I thought you knew better. A séance?"

"Séances are fun," I said weakly. Or at least they seemed that way on TV. This was the first I'd ever been to, and it had been anything but.

"Séances are dangerous," he corrected. "You have to do them *properly*."

"For someone who sneers at seances, you seem to know a lot about them."

"Forget the ghosties." He glanced around and lowered his voice. "I *can* tell you that Lizzy Barnhart has a JustGroupies page."

My forehead creased. "A what?"

"You know, an account where people pay to see saucy pictures."

Good Lord. Dirty pictures? "Lizzy's doing—?"

"Regency-era ankles."

I blinked. "What?" That was a thing?

"Well, the feet are attached, of course. And you know how some men are about feet." He rolled his eyes.

"Ah..." No. "Is the account under her name?"

"Of course not. She has a pseudonym, Lady Anklesford. She only started up recently, but I can see she's going places. Her views are trending upward. Sorry, as gossip goes, it's not much. No one *cares* about dirty pictures these days, especially ankle shots. No one has *standards* anymore."

"No," I murmured.

The bell over the blue front door jingled. Martin Carlton, in a brown suit and skinny slacks, minced into the tearoom and scanned the crowd. Spotting me, he beelined for the counter. "Abigail, right? May we have a chat? About Saturday?"

Archer swiveled on his stool, his eyes lighting. "And who is this?"

"No one," I said. Archer had done me a solid with the Lady Anklesford lead, but it wouldn't be right to inflict Archer's gossip column on Martin.

Martin stuck his hand out. "Martin Carlton."

I smothered a groan. Once Archer had a name, he was relentless.

"Community Liaison for Benson Investments," Martin continued.

I sucked in a breath. "Benson? As in, *Derek* Benson?" Martin had *worked* for the murdered man? Was that how he'd become group moderator for their fanfic chat?

"The same." Martin smiled briefly.

Archer angled his silvery head to one side. "I heard Derek was having some trouble with the City Council about a development north of the Yacht Club."

Or maybe I could let Archer go to town and see what we learned. I braced an elbow on the counter and smiled expectantly.

Martin stiffened. "Not exactly trouble, no."

"Then *exactly* what?" Archer asked.

Martin turned to me. "Abigail, may I speak to you privately?"

"When we were getting along so well?" Archer made a tsking sound.

Darn it. "I guess. See ya, Archer." I moved around the counter and into the hallway. "I heard you're the moderator for the Austen fan-fic group."

"Yes." Martin preened. "I was the obvious choice."

I stopped beside Hyperion's door. The twinkle lights flashed erratically. "Why did you delete all the chats?" I lowered my head to study him.

"Because it wasn't seemly to keep them up. Derek is dead. We don't want the press digging up his Jane Austen obsession. He could get rather... heated on the topic."

I knocked on Hyperion's office door, though I was pretty sure he didn't have a client in there. He usually didn't see clients until later in the afternoon.

"Enter," Hyperion intoned.

Suppressing an eye roll, I walked inside.

Martin took a hesitant step into Hyperion's office. His gaze darted to the driftwood altar, the tabby atop it, the high-backed, red velvet chairs. "It's a very *private* matter," he told me.

"Then Hyperion should definitely be involved." What did Martin want with me? *Hyperion* had been lord of the séance.

"Take a load off." Hyperion shut his laptop and motioned toward the matching chair opposite.

Martin took one slow step toward the chair, then another, then finally, he pulled it back and sat. I shut the door and leaned against it.

"I wanted a *woman's* advice," Martin said.

Hyperion cocked a brow. "Why? I'm a Tarot reader. That's even better."

"He's good at advising," I agreed.

Martin sneezed. "I have great respect for Mrs. Landsford."

"Kathy? Why?" I asked. I wasn't trying to be catty. I really wanted to know.

Martin twisted, leaning over the arm of his chair to see me. "She's a tremendous force in the community, and a masterful writer. No one appreciates Jane Austen more than she."

"But you're afraid she murdered your boss?" I asked.

His hazel eyes widened. "No," he said explosively. "Of course not. A woman like that would never— But I don't want her to be blamed."

"Blamed for what?" I asked.

His gaze lowered. "Ah. I'm simply a community liaison. I don't know much about Derek's private life."

"But?" Hyperion prompted.

"But as community liaison, I hear certain things."

Hyperion braced his elbows on the red-clothed table. "Such as?"

The tabby hopped down from the table and strode purposefully toward Martin's ankles.

Martin studied the cat with an expression of fascinated horror. "Er, it falls into the shameless gossip category, unfortunately. That's why I wasn't sure if I should tell the police."

"You should," I said.

Hyperion motioned negligently. "Yes, yes. But there's no reason you can't tell us first."

There were plenty of reasons. And I kept that thought to myself.

Bastet rubbed against Martin's leg, depositing several orange hairs on his brown slacks. Why were cats so fascinated by people who obviously disliked them?

Martin straightened in his chair. "Lizzy Barnhart has been bad mouthing Derek's investments. That's the little, er, trouble that your... friend just mentioned. *She* has a friend on the city council."

"Bad mouthing how?" And what did that have to do with Kathy?

"Apparently..." Martin edged his foot away from the tabby. "And I wouldn't bring this up at all if it weren't for Mrs. Landsford. She's been through so much already, what with her most recent husband dying, and all the responsibilities she's had to take on with their charities."

Bastet batted at the tassels on Martin's loafers.

"Bring what up?" Hyperion asked.

"TalesTrove.com was an anomaly for Benson Investments. Our investment group pools investments from qualified individuals and then usually purchases property to build on. After roughly five years, we sell the finished properties, preferably at a profit for the qualified investors."

"What makes a qualified investor?" I asked.

"It's an FTC rule. One needs an income of over $200,000 or net worth of over a million, not including one's personal residence," he said promptly. "Lizzy qualified—"

"Lizzy has that much money?" I asked, straightening off the door.

Martin crimsoned. "Erm, no. Not anymore. She'd inherited money from her family, and then invested it. Unfortunately, that investment didn't really work out."

"How did she get in on this?" Hyperion asked.

Martin's flush deepened. "Uh. Rumor has it that she and Derek were romantically involved. It's only rumor," he added quickly. "But it would explain why she's been so, er, vehement."

"Losing the family fortune might have had something to do with her vehemence," I said dryly. And the relationship was more than rumor. Lizzy had admitted to it.

The door bounced against my back. I stepped aside, turning.

"I can see that everyone at the séance is a suspect," Martin said. "I don't want to point the police at Lizzy, but Mrs. Landsford shouldn't be subjected to this."

"Subjected to what?" Kathy boomed. Bastet and I started.

My grandfather opened the door wider. "Sorry to interrupt," he said, clutching his cabby hat in one hand. He stuffed it into the pocket of his tan sports jacket.

I narrowed my eyes. What were those two doing together?

"Subjected to what?" the older woman repeated. She wore an elegant, hip-length ivory coat over gray slacks and a matching sequined top.

"The police," Martin bleated, leaping from his chair.

"Oh. Them." She tossed her mercury hair and took Martin's red-velvet chair. "It's highly unlikely *I'm* a suspect. What are you really doing here, Martin?"

"Nothing," he squeaked, shrinking.

My neck stiffened. "What are *you* doing here?" I asked her.

"I had intended to compare notes on Derek's murder." She plucked at a sequin. "Now that Martin is here, I see no reason why I should alter that plan. Martin, what did you see the night of the séance?"

The little man looked about wildly. "Nothing, nothing. I was blinded like everyone else when that candle went out."

"And did you hear anything?" she insisted.

"Nothing," Martin said. "I thought… I thought I *might* have detected some movement across the table—"

"Earlier, you said you didn't see anything," Kathy barked.

"Maybe just a shape, I couldn't be sure…" he trailed off.

"What did you see?" Hyperion asked her.

"Not a damned thing." She crossed one leg over the other, bouncing her foot. "Didn't hear anything either. I'm afraid my hearing isn't what it was."

"It would have taken some strength, I would think, to drive a dagger into Derek," Martin said. "No alliteration intended."

"Nonsense," Kathy said. "Quick upward strikes into his lower torso?" She shook her head. "Lots of soft tissue and unprotected organs there. When I was young, I worked as a candy striper, you know. Heard lots of things from the doctors. Anyone could have done it. Well, most anyone."

My pulse quickened, the blood throbbing in my skull. How did everyone know so much about shanking? Was it going to overtake axe throwing as the next trendy hobby?

Hyperion tented his fingers. "There's someone you've crossed off the suspect list?"

"Giorgi." Kathy's smile was wintery. "I can't see him stabbing someone. The boy is pretty but useless. Lovely penmanship though."

"But *you* could have killed Derek?" I asked.

"Of course," she said. "Not that I *would* have killed Derek. I want Jane's letter, but not enough to murder my rival. That wouldn't be fair play." She rose and smiled at my grandfather. "You understand."

Gramps shrugged. "I wouldn't kill over a letter either."

"Who knew you were bringing a real candle to the séance?" I asked.

"The invitation was for a candlelit séance at Beanblossom's Tea and Tarot," she said. "So, one would presume, everybody knew. Would you mind if we left now?" she asked my grandfather.

"Of course not," he said, and she took his arm.

Uneasy, I followed the two down the hallway to the rear entrance. "Kathy, who do you think might have killed Derek?"

My grandfather opened the heavy, metal door for her. I winced at the sunlight.

"Derek was not a very nice man." She stepped into the parking lot. "He certainly wasn't kind to Martin."

"Oh?" I trailed the two of them into the parking lot.

She wrinkled her nose at a dumpster as we passed. "Martin thought he could do more at the company, but he's only good at being obsequious. Derek recognized that. However, he refused to tell that to the poor man. Martin actually believed he'd be promoted to a management position."

"Did you invite Derek to the séance?" I asked.

"Hardly," she said. "That was Martin's doing. He informed me Derek was coming, and I got the word out. I thought the others should be warned. Feelings are running high about the website's new AI component."

We walked toward my hatchback. Parked beside it was a forest-green—I gaped. Was that actually a Rolls Royce?

Grinning, my grandfather opened its passenger door for Kathy. She slowly got inside, swiveling both her legs in together.

My grandfather walked to the driver's side.

"Gramps? Are you driving this?" I whispered.

His grin widened. "She asked me to. How could I say *no*?"

"I didn't think you were a car guy."

"It's a Rolls Royce. Everyone's a car guy when a Rolls is involved."

No argument there. I wanted to give it a spin. I glanced back at the tearoom. No. Things were busy. I couldn't ask if they could give me a ride.

Regretfully, I stepped from the car. My grandfather grunted, lowering himself onto the sand-colored leather seat.

"Well," I said, "if you—"

CRACK. PING.

The side mirror on the Rolls jerked.

CRASH.

"Abigail, get down," my grandfather shouted.

I dropped to the pavement, heart banging against my ribs. Someone had taken a shot at us.

Chapter 8

Realizing someone's shooting at you is, to put it mildly, alarming. It's worse when you realize they may be shooting at someone you love. That's not just a wake-up call; it's a "get out of bed or die trying" siren.

I crouched beside the Rolls, my heart hammering. Hunched low in the driver's seat, my grandfather met my gaze. His blue eyes blazed.

"What happened?" Kathy demanded, gripping the sleeve of his tan jacket. "What's happening? What happened to my car?"

"Get down," my grandfather said. "Someone's got a gun."

Instead of getting down, Kathy scooted closer to him. "Nonsense. That was a dueling pistol." Reaching across my grandfather, she cranked down the driver's side window.

Gramps craned his neck, amazement scrawled across his face. "You could tell that from the sound?"

"Of course not. I saw the muzzle flash beside that dumpster. There." She pointed behind us to the dumpster by Beanblossom's. "As that was a single-shot flintlock, one would assume the attacker has one shot, unless he also has the loaded partner to this pistol. That would give him one more. But there are three of us."

I squinted up at her. "Yeah, but I'd rather *none* of us get shot."

She snorted. Her head vanished from the window.

"I'm calling the cops." My grandfather pulled his flip phone from the pocket of his sports jacket.

A Honda Civic drifted behind the Rolls. It stopped, and a florid faced, middle-aged man leaned out the open window. He whistled. "Is that a Rolls?" The man squinted at me. "What are you doing on the ground?"

A car door snicked open. "Yes, it is, young man," Kathy said. Her heels clicked on the pavement. "Please remain parked there. Someone took a shot at me. I need a buffer."

The man blinked. "Uh... What?"

She strode around her car's glittering fender and frowned down at me. "Really. Whoever took the shot is long gone. You can get up now."

"Then why do you need a buffer?" Embarrassed, I scrambled to standing. Gramps took a bit longer extricating himself from the Rolls.

"There could be a second shooter," she said.

"What does a car like that go for?" the man in the Honda asked.

Kathy sniffed. "You couldn't afford the gas."

The man's face pinched. The Honda roared off.

"It gets five miles per gallon," Gramps murmured. "I couldn't afford the gas."

While we waited for the police, I walked around the Rolls. I'd swear I'd heard glass breaking...

I sucked in an angry breath. The passenger side window of my Mazda hatchback was a spiderweb of broken glass. The bullet must have ricocheted.

My grandfather sighed. "Your insurance isn't going to like that."

"Forget my insurance. If the bullet's inside, the cops could impound my car." I unlocked the passenger side door and opened it, leaning my head inside. A misshapen piece of lead lay on the passenger seat.

I touched the scuff on the back of my headrest. "Weird. It didn't go through."

"It couldn't," Kathy said. "Dueling pistols are meant for shots twenty-five or thirty feet away. As I suspected, this was a flintlock, twenty-eight-bore, and roughly fifty to fifty-five calibers." She reached for the lump of metal.

"Don't touch that," Gramps and I shouted simultaneously.

She jerked her hand away and glared. "Really."

"Sorry," he told her. "Your knowledge of dueling pistols is impressive, but unfortunately, I have a good bit of knowledge about police procedures."

She raised her silvery brows. "As an accountant?"

"As Abigail's grandfather."

"The *point*," Kathy continued, "is that when the bullet struck my car, it slowed, bent, and tumbled, and when it struck this window, it slowed even more."

"You *do* know a lot about dueling pistols," I said. She might be bossy, but at least she was smart. I didn't know if that should relieve me or make me more worried.

"Dueling was a nasty business," she said. "But I believe if one is going to study a period in time, one should do it *well*."

"You said you saw a muzzle flash," I said. "Did you get a look at who was holding the gun?"

Kathy shook her head. "No. I was too busy ducking."

"Intelligent woman," my grandfather said, and she smiled.

Baranko arrived shortly thereafter. He wasn't happy, but he didn't take us downtown. We all returned inside while he used a laser pointer to try and calculate the lead ball's trajectory.

Kathy flung open the door to Hyperion's office. "Where is he?"

Bastet twitched on the driftwood altar. The tabby's ears flattened.

Hyperion looked up from his laptop. "Where's who?"

A single Tarot card lay face up on the table's crimson cloth. It was the Tower, a card of sudden, unexpected disaster. The kicker is that the disaster's only unexpected because you weren't paying attention.

I pursed my lips. The card seemed a little personal.

Kathy jammed her hands on the hips of her soft ivory coat. "Martin."

"Uh..." Hyperion looked around. "He left."

"I can see that, young man. When did he leave? Where did he go?"

"He left right after you did, and I have no idea where he went." Hyperion checked his watch. "Why?"

"That rotten bootlicker," Kathy hissed. "Martin tried to kill me. And I'm quite certain he uses AI to write his stories."

"Someone took a shot at us in the parking lot," I explained.

"Is everyone okay?" Hyperion jerked forward in his high-backed chair. "Because you seem okay. Why didn't I hear the shot?"

"They used a dueling pistol," I said.

Gramps removed his cabby hat and smoothed wisps of white hair over his head. "We're fine."

"How do you know it was a dueling pistol?" Hyperion asked. "Did they leave the pistol behind?"

"No," I said. "Kathy identified it by the muzzle flash and by the bullet left in my car."

Hyperion's brow furrowed. "Muzzle? Do dueling pistols use bullets, or something else?"

"They may be called lead balls or bullets." Kathy patted her silver hair.

"I don't remember any dueling in Jane Austen." Hyperion angled his head.

"Mrs. Bennet in *Pride and Prejudice* said she was afraid Mr. Bennet would fight Mr. Wickham," Gramps said.

"And Colonel Brandon and Mr. Willoughby dueled in *Sense and Sensibility*," Kathy said, not to be outdone. "Jane never specified if the duel was fought with swords or guns, but pistols were the weapon of choice in England by the 1770s. *Sense and Sensibility* was published in three volumes in 1811."

"Fascinating," Hyperion said faintly.

"It really is," my grandfather said. "Once you start digging into the details of her books, it opens up the history of that period in all sorts of ways."

"We're wasting time," Kathy said. "Martin needs to be arrested."

"Hold on," I said. "Just because he had—"

"Means, motive, and opportunity?" Kathy asked, caustic.

"What's his motive?" I asked her.

"He hated Derek for dangling that promotion in front of him and giving it to someone else. I'm going to tell that detective." She stormed from the office.

The tearoom's rear door slammed, echoing down the hallway outside.

"You two are really okay?" Hyperion asked.

"Not even a scratch," Gramps said.

"Because you have what looks like oil on the back of your pants," Hyperion told me.

I twisted. "Darn it." I must have leaned against a tire or something. "I did learn something earlier I forgot to mention. Archer was here looking for gossip. He said Lizzy has a Regency-era JustGroupies page."

"Sexy corset shots?" Hyperion waggled his brows. My grandfather pinked.

"Ankles," I said.

My partner blinked. "Okaaaay." He pulled the laptop to him and typed. Gramps and I grouped around his velvet chair. "And I thought a Jane Austen séance would be elegant and genteel," he muttered. "These people are obsessed."

An image of a woman's hands clutching the raised hem of a dress to expose a silk-clad foot and ankle appeared on the screen.

"It's not exactly blackmail worthy," Hyperion said.

"She's got a nice ankle though," Gramps said.

"Does it say how many followers she has?" I asked.

"Forty-two," Hyperion said. "But she only started the page a couple months ago."

"Is that the only photo?" Gramps asked.

"I'd guess not." Hyperion crossed his arms over his chest. "But I'd have to pay twenty-five bucks to see more."

"For an ankle?" My grandfather's snowy eyebrows shot skyward.

I gnawed my bottom lip. "I'll pay it." I was already over my incidentals budget for the month. But the month was nearly over, and we needed to know.

"For an *ankle*?" my grandfather repeated.

I got my purse from the kitchen, pulled out my wallet, and handed Hyperion my credit card. "Just make sure I'm not stuck with a subscription."

He nodded and started typing. A minute later, we'd accessed a page-full of ankle photos.

Hyperion scrolled down.

"Stop," I said.

He lifted his hands off the keyboard.

"Go back," I said.

He scrolled up.

"There," I said. "Click that picture."

He did, and it expanded. A photo of Lizzy exposing a slippered foot, an ankle covered by her silk stocking. In her hand was an antique quill knife.

Chapter 9

I GASPED, LEANING CLOSER to the screen of Hyperion's laptop. "Is that—?"

"The same knife," Gramps said heavily. "It looks just like the murder weapon."

Bastet hopped down from his spot on the driftwood altar. The tabby ambled toward us.

My jaw slackened. "She couldn't possibly be that stupid," I said, "could she?" Using a weapon she'd photographed herself with to kill a man?

Hyperion folded his arms. "People can be pretty stupid."

"I know," I said, "but *that* stupid?"

"I can't believe Lizzy did it," Gramps said. "She's a smart girl, er, woman. All of the people in our group are intelligent. They couldn't write as well if..." His brows drew together. "Well, Martin's writing has dramatically improved since the AI came online, but still. It's too obvious."

"And sometimes the simplest answer is the correct one," I said.

Hyperion's office door clicked open. He slammed down the lid of the laptop. The deck of Tarot cards beside it slid sideways on the red-clothed table.

Razzzor stood in the doorway. He shoved his wire-frame glasses higher up his nose. "What are all those cops doing in your parking lot?"

His brown hair was rumpled, and his skin had the pallor of a man whose only exposure to light was a computer screen. His Hawaiian shirt was untucked over his jeans. Razzzor was successful, so the outfit managed to look stylish on his wiry frame.

"Someone took a shot at us with a dueling pistol," I said. "No one was hurt."

Razzzor's jaw tightened. "That does it. Forget HR. I'm in. Was he shooting at you and Hyperion?"

"Me, Gramps, and Kathy," I said. "We don't know who the actual target was."

"I don't know why anyone would be shooting at Kathy," Gramps said. "If she saw anything at the séance, she'd have told the police."

"Kathy Landsford?" Razzzor asked, and we nodded. "Well, she's wealthy. And her last two husbands died under sort of suspicious circumstances, but—"

"What?" Fingering my jade pendant, I glanced at my grandfather. "Why didn't you mention that before?"

Razzzor's pale skin flushed. "I thought you knew. One guy fell off a boat, and the other slipped while mountain climbing."

"Tragic," my grandfather muttered. "She's been through a lot."

"*Two* deadly falls?" I tried not to look at my grandfather.

"She's either unlucky or a black widow," Hyperion said. "Whoever falls for her literally takes a fall. One push down the stairs and…" He made a twisting motion with his hands.

My grandfather frowned.

"Were her husbands wealthy?" I asked Razzzor.

"Big time," he said.

That was a relief. My grandfather was at the low-end of the upper middle class—which in Silicon Valley meant financially challenged. If Kathy was hunting for another wealthy husband, Gramps was out of the running.

"What are you doing here?" I asked Razzzor. Visits IRL from my ex-boss were rare. He was a busy guy and preferred the heady aether of the online world.

"Ah…" He glanced at my grandfather. "Maybe we should talk privately."

I motioned at Gramps. "It's okay. He knows everything."

Gramps flicked his gaze to the white ceiling.

"It's, um, about Lizzy." Razzzor shuffled his feet.

"What about her?" I asked.

Razzzor's face took on an even redder hue. "Um..." His gaze darted to my grandfather and then to the laptop. "You see, there's this, uh, website, called JustGroupies—"

"The ankle pics?" Hyperion made a dismissive motion. "Old news."

"You know?" Razzzor sputtered. "How?"

"A simple web search," Hyperion said loftily.

"Okay, fine," Razzzor said, miffed. "Do you know about the air cannon found in the dead man's pocket?"

"A what?" I asked.

"Air cannon. Simple design," Razzzor said. "You just pull it back, the rubber snaps, and it puffs out air. It's pretty quiet and can get decent range. I watched a video online where someone made one to blow out a kid's birthday candles."

"So that was how the candle was blown out at the séance," I said. "Assuming Derek didn't blow it out, the killer must have planted the cannon in his pocket?"

"Assuming?" Hyperion asked. "Why would *Derek* blow out the candle?"

My face heated. "I don't know. I'm just trying to cover all possibilities. I'm brainstorming. You said there's a snapping sound. Did anyone hear that?"

"I might have," Hyperion said. "But I can't be sure."

"I heard a whooshing noise, not a snap," Gramps said. "But my hearing's not as good as it was."

On the altar, Bastet stretched. A quartz crystal dropped to the carpet. The tabby jerked at the sound and leapt from his perch. Tail bushy, he ran beneath the round table, rustling the crimson tablecloth.

"It'd be a snap then a whoosh." Razzzor rubbed his chin. "Who had the opportunity to plant the air cannon in Derek's pocket?"

"Lizzy," I said. "She was sitting right beside him. Giorgi helped move him, so he's a possible. And Kathy touched him too." I glanced at my grandfather.

"And me," Gramps said heavily.

Beneath the table, the cat howled.

"No one thinks you did it," I told my grandfather.

"But I was sitting right beside Derek," Gramps said. "The police have to consider me a suspect."

"What possible motive could you have?" Hyperion asked curiously.

Gramps shuffled his feet. "I was kind of outspoken about the introduction of AI into the website. Having AI write your story doesn't seem like real art or literature. There's no soul behind it. It's entirely mechanistic."

"AI's taking over everything," I said, glum. I hated it. I wanted to deal with humans, not bots. I wanted to enjoy paintings and writing written by *people*.

"It's not taking over *everything*," Razzzor said.

"Yeah," Hyperion said. "It'll never take the place of a Tarot reader."

"I suppose it could though." Razzzor's pale brow furrowed. "I mean, a true random number generator really is a message from the universe."

"How?" Hyperion's expressive face pinched with disdain.

"It's a string of ones and zeroes." Razzzor rubbed his chin. "Who or what determines that? The universe. The consciousness involved would be the person asking the question, and the universe gives the answer. Then the AI could interpret it. Theoretically, it's possible. In fact—"

"No," Hyperion said flatly. "Don't even think about it."

"I'm just saying—"

Hyperion jolted straighter in his chair. "NO."

An awkward silence fell. "I'm sure most people will still want the human touch," I ventured.

Hyperion glared. "*Most* people?"

"I don't suppose Martin could have used the cannon," Gramps said. "He never got near Derek to plant it in his pocket after he fell forward."

"Unless Martin was the killer," I said. "If he snuck around to stab him, he could have planted the air cannon then."

"That's a lot to do in the dark and not much time to do it," Hyperion said.

My mouth twisted. Hyperion was right. It would be difficult. But not impossible. "So you're suggesting the cannon was planted in the confusion *after* Derek had been stabbed?"

"I think it makes the most sense," Hyperion said.

Slowly, I nodded. It made sense to me too. And Lizzy had been right beside Derek. "Do you know which pocket they found the cannon in?" I asked Razzzor.

"Left jacket pocket," he said.

"And Lizzy was on Derek's left," Gramps said heavily. "We need to talk to her."

"If the police haven't already," I said.

"Cool," Razzzor said. "Oh, one more thing. I dug into that fan-fic website. Rumor has it the whole thing was Giorgi Westen's idea, but Derek Bensen somehow got his name, and his name alone, on the patent."

"Giorgi already told us he got bounced out of the project," Hyperion said.

"Then my work here is done." Razzzor strode from the office.

I hurried into the hallway after him. "Hey, wait up." Hyperion's door clicked shut behind me.

Razzzor's lanky figure stopped beside the tearoom's rear, metal door. "What's up?"

"I dunno. Just... thanks."

He saluted with his forefinger. "Anything for the cause of Lady Justice."

"Yeah," I said. "But thanks anyway."

He squinted at me. "You okay?"

"Yeah. I mean, I'm a little worried about my grandfather, but—"

"Why?" He adjusted his glasses. "There's no way they'll arrest him for murder."

"I'm more worried about him becoming a victim," I muttered. *Of Kathy.*

"What?"

"Nothing." I shook my head. "Just...could you dig a little deeper into the deaths of Kathy's husbands?"

"Sure. No problem."

He walked outside, and the sunlight streaming through the door briefly blinded me. The door clanged shut, leaving me rubbing my eyes.

Blinking, I returned down the hallway to Hyperion's door and to my grandfather. The twinkle lights winked dismally, and my chest tightened. Was I going too far trying to protect my grandfather?

I paused, one hand on the doorknob, and pressed my lips together. No. One man was dead. Kathy was a murder suspect. I probably wasn't going far enough.

The door opened beneath my fingers. I jerked my hand away.

"You ready?" Hyperion shrugged into his green suit jacket.

"For what?" I asked.

"We're headed back to Lizzy's." He stepped into the hallway.

My grandfather followed, adjusting the cabbie hat on his head. "To the theater, he means."

"The theater with the ostriches?" I asked. "How do you know she's there?"

"She posted a pic from her dressing room an hour ago," Hyperion said. "Natch."

"Natch," I said dryly.

"They're prepping for tonight's show," Gramps said. "The director wants some changes."

I hesitated. It was Tuesday, and the tearoom was hopping. But I wasn't going to leave Gramps and Hyperion to investigate on their own. Hurrying to the kitchen, I pulled off my sunflower apron and told Maricel we were leaving.

My manager twisted her hands in her apron. Above it, her t-shirt proclaimed: *Oxford Comma Enthusiast*. "You're leaving? Now?"

Heat scorched my face. What was I doing? I couldn't just take off in the middle of the day. Beanblossom's was busy. "You don't want me to leave. It's fine. I'll tell Hyperion—"

"No, no. It's not..." Her olive skin darkened. "It's silly, but, have you noticed anything... strange since the séance?"

"Ah..." I rubbed my cheek. "The only thing strange was the murder, which would be better described as awful."

"I know," she said in a rush. "I can't stop thinking about it. No one can. Maybe *that's* why we're seeing things where there aren't any."

Okaaay. "Seeing... uh, what exactly?"

Maricel tugged on the end of her long, black braid. "Sierra swears she saw a teacup move across the counter on its own."

"It was probably vibration from a passing truck. You know how that can jiggle the counter. Or maybe the cup was sitting in a pool of water and just slid."

"It's not just that. The shadows in the hallway are…" Maricel glanced toward the open kitchen door. "They're not right."

"Could there be a problem with the lights?"

"Yes, sometimes they flicker," she said in a rush. "It started today. Or maybe Monday, I don't know, because Beanblossom's was closed then. But there've been cold spots, and… People think the tearoom is haunted."

My shoulders curled inward, toward the tingling in my chest. "Haunted." I should have expected this. People were probably taking pictures in the tearoom hoping they'd catch orbs.

"Did you, er, close the séance?" Maricel asked.

"Close it?" I asked blankly. The séance had ended with Derek's murder. What was to close?

"After you summon a spirit, you need to dismiss it. That's what one of the Tarot readers said. We were just thinking because someone died, maybe you, ah, didn't?"

We hadn't. Not that I believed… Hell, I wasn't sure what I believed. Were there things we didn't understand? *Definitely*. Was there more out there than our senses could perceive? *Probably*. But not every bump in the night was a ghost.

A dull weight pressed against my chest. "I shouldn't have opened Beanblossom's today," I said heavily. "Not so soon after the murder." What had I been thinking?

"I don't think anyone thinks you did anything wrong. I mean, no one's judging you for that."

I was judging me. But we'd had reservations, and I hated canceling reservations. Not because of the money, because it was rude, especially at the last minute.

"It's probably…" I didn't want to say mass hysteria. That was just insulting. "People are on edge. If people think it's the ghost of the murdered man…" I swallowed. Was it possible? "I don't think ghosts can manifest that quickly. Can they?"

"What if it isn't the ghost of the murdered man. What if it's something... else?"

I ran my finger along my necklace chain. No. I was not going down this path. I nodded curtly. "Then we'll deal with it. Between all the psychic knowledge at Beanblossom's, there's got to be a solution."

Maricel released a gusty breath. "Right. Right. We'll figure this out. It's not like anyone's been hurt."

Aside from Derek. "We'll sort it out," I agreed before she could worry that Derek's murder might have been the result of a malevolent spirit. *Or worse.*

She smiled slowly. "Great. Thanks."

I hurried to the parking lot. Baranko was gone, which was a relief. Even more of a relief, my Mazda with its broken window was still there. He hadn't impounded it.

"What took you so long?" Hyperion started the ignition on his yellow Jeep.

"The staff wants to know if we closed the séance." In the back seat, I buckled my belt.

Hyperion's head turned. He met my gaze. "Oh, hell."

"Wait." I froze, one hand still on the buckle. "That's really a thing?"

"What do you mean, close it?" Gramps asked.

"We opened the séance to spirits," Hyperion said, "but we never closed the portal. I forgot. But the police were there, and what was I *supposed* to do?"

My stomach hit my sneakers. "So that really *is* a thing? You're not just pulling my leg?"

Hyperion rubbed his jaw. "It's, uh... fine." He backed from the spot. "We'll just do it tonight."

"And that'll work?" I asked. "I mean, I'm not sure I believe in all that or anything, but the staff does. We have to do it right."

"Why?" Gramps asked. "What's the problem?"

I cleared my throat. "Some people, ah, think the tearoom's haunted."

Hyperion braked hard, flinging us against our seatbelts. "How haunted?"

"What do you mean, 'how haunted?'" I asked. "Haunted is haunted."

"No, no, no." Hyperion shook his head. "There's delightfully haunted, the sort of haunted that brings in business. And then there's demonically haunted, where people find three-clawed scratches on their backs and only goths and ghosthunters dine in."

"No one's been hurt," I said. *Except for Derek.* "Derek wasn't killed by a demon, he was killed by a human." Clutching my arms to my chest, I pressed deeper into my seat.

Hyperion's shoulders hunched. "Right, right." He put the Jeep in gear, and we drove in silence to the theater.

I was freaking myself out. I could not afford to freak myself out. Not now. Not with a tearoom to run and a killer on the loose.

We turned off the highway and bumped down the dirt road toward the theater. Ostriches clustered at the far end of the field, away from the barn.

I shrank, my insides rolling. The birds had no doubt been scared off by the flashing blue lights of the police cars surrounding the theater. A coroner's van stood off to one side.

Chapter 10

Lizzy was dead.

Lizzy was dead, and we'd been wrong, and could I have stopped it? I squeezed my eyes shut. Could I have listened more and spoken less? Could I have spoken better and convinced her to tell us more? Could any of us have done more?

Detective Baranko didn't take us down to the station. He separated us and had his minions do the interviews in the theater's red barn.

Except for my interview. Baranko got me all to himself.

I was a witness and not a suspect. So, I told him everything I knew, finishing with the JustGroupies page and the quill knife.

His beady eyes widened briefly when I told him about Lady Anklesford. Then he returned to his usual glowering. "What else?"

Lizzy was dead, and I was having a hard time breathing. I wouldn't leave anything out. "Nothing else." I slumped in one of the theater's folding metal chairs.

"Why'd you come to the theater?" he asked.

I looked toward the stage, where a cop interviewed my grandfather. Okay, I wasn't going to leave anything out except *this*. If I told him we'd come to ask about the quill knife, would that be interfering in an investigation?

On the other hand, if Hyperion and Gramps were giving the cops the whole truth and nothing but the truth...

I rubbed my chin. "You know, we didn't discuss our goals. Hyperion told me they were going to the Ostrich Theater and asked if I wanted to come along."

Baranko's eyes narrowed. "So, you abandoned your tearoom just to come to the theater, without having any clear goals in mind?"

I nodded. "Yeah. That's what happened."

"And the attack with the dueling pistol?"

"We called you about that," I said quickly. "You know everything about the gunshot that we do."

"What I know is you're sticking your nose in another murder investigation."

"It's a small town," I said weakly. "Everyone's asking about it."

"*Everyone* isn't getting shot at."

"It was Kathy's Rolls that got hit first," I pointed out. "It's not my fault the bullet ricocheted into mine."

"You were standing next to her car. What aren't you telling me?"

"Nothing." I'd told him everything—probably more than I should have. But Lizzy was dead, and my gut twisted sickeningly.

Eventually, Baranko let me go. I wandered outside and to the high, wire fence where the ostriches had stood. One pecked at the ground on the far side of the field.

Lizzy's knife. She must have recognized it when Derek was killed. That would explain some of her agitation, her anxiety. Had she suspected who'd used it to kill? But why not tell the police?

A woman in jeans and a checked red shirt came to lounge against the fence beside me. "You talk to the cops yet?" she asked.

"Yeah," I said. "You?"

The ostrich strutted into a stand of Eucalyptus trees and vanished.

"They just let me go," she said. "I'm not sure where to go now. They'll probably cancel tonight's show, but in case they don't, I have to stick around."

"How can you rehearse without Lizzy?"

She flushed. "I'm her understudy."

"Oh."

"But I didn't kill her for the part," she said hastily. "I mean, come on. The Ostrich Theater isn't exactly worth a murder."

We didn't say anything for a while. The September air was cool on my face and damp with a hint of the Pacific. The field behind the actress was empty and green. A bank of fog lay gray along the horizon. And I'd been wrong about everything.

"I'm sorry for your loss," I finally said.

"I'm sorry I found the body." She hugged herself. "It was awful."

"What?" If she'd found the body... This was exactly the wrong time for me to ask her about it. But I *had* to ask. "What happened?"

She straightened, shifting nervously.

"Have you been interviewed?" Baranko bellowed, pointing at us from his spot beside a squad car.

"Yeah," the woman shouted back. "They told me I could go."

"Then go," he said and turned away.

Her shoulders hunched, and she leaned against the wire fence. "I can't go," she told me miserably. "Not until I know what's going on."

"Do you have any idea what happened to Lizzy?" I asked.

"I think she shot herself," she said slowly and looked away. "There was a lot of blood. And an old-timey gun was beside her hand on the floor."

I felt the blood drain from my face. "Old timey? Like, a dueling pistol?"

"I guess." She shrugged. "I don't know."

"I'm sorry," I said in a low voice. I was glad I hadn't found the body. I wouldn't have wanted to see Lizzy that way. And then I felt guilty for being glad. "I'm Abigail, by the way."

"Sandra," she said.

"Were you—?"

"Are you talking to her?" Baranko strode toward us, the hems of his trench coat flapping. "Stop talking to her." He stabbed a thick finger in my direction.

"I'm waiting to talk to the director," the woman said. "I can't leave without her permission. We were about to start going over tonight's changes."

"Who's the director?" Baranko asked.

"Bellamy," she said.

The detective swore. "I'll talk to her. You." He pointed at me. "Go stand over there." He nodded to Hyperion's Jeep, parked on the side of the dirt driveway.

"You," he told Sandra. "Stay by the fence."

He watched me trudge to the yellow Jeep. I folded my arms and leaned against a passenger door.

The detective strode toward the barn, his trench coat flapping. He vanished inside.

I walked to the Jeep's front bumper. Sandra edged along the wire fence line toward me until we stood only ten feet apart. "He didn't say *where* by the fence I had to stand," she said.

I nodded. "Clarity in direction is important."

"I saw you around the theater before." Sandra squinted at me. "How do you know Lizzy?"

Two ostriches wandered around the corner of the barn. One wore a green scarf tied jauntily around its neck.

"I'm part owner at the tearoom where the séance was being run, er, facilitated," I said. "You know, where Derek Benson was killed? My partner was facilitating the séance."

"So... you don't really know her?"

"No, not really. But a man died in my tearoom, and I guess I'm just trying to make sense of it."

"It's the bargaining stage of grief." Sandra shivered. "Sense making."

"Except I'm not grieving," I said, though a part of me was for Lizzy. *Grief and guilt, the worst combination.* "I didn't know Derek. I'm just... It's just wrong. Murder is wrong. Using my tearoom to do it was wrong."

I hadn't known Lizzy well either. But my brain revolted against the idea that she was gone. My fists clenched at my sides.

Sandra lowered her head. "What happened to Lizzy was wrong. She was no saint, but... suicide? Someone pushed her to do it. Maybe it was this Derek guy, maybe someone else." She shuddered. "I can't believe she did it."

"Did you hear a gunshot?"

Sandra nodded. "There was a bang, but we didn't really think anything of it. It was faint, and things are always banging around in the theater."

"What time did you hear the bang?" I asked.

"Sometime before two, before we were supposed to start."

A yellow sheet of paper fluttered across the road. The wind plastered it to the wire fence where Sandra and I had stood.

"Do you know what time Lizzy got to the theater today?" I asked.

"We arrived at the same time, around one-thirty." She nodded to a battered Honda Civic besides an ancient VW van. "The van's mine. The Civic is—was—Lizzy's. She went backstage to change. I stopped to talk to the director. When I went backstage, I didn't see her, but I figured she was in the ladies room. And then rehearsal started at two, and she wasn't there. So, I checked the ladies room."

"You found her there?" I guessed.

"Yeah." Sandra blinked rapidly.

"Were you two close?" I asked quietly.

"No. She didn't talk a lot about herself. Lizzy was a real pro."

A gust of wind tossed my hair. It plucked the yellow paper from the grass and blew it to stop at my khaki sneakers. I bent and picked it up.

It was a playbill for *Sense and Sensibility*. Lizzy's name had top billing. I flipped to its back side and sucked in a breath. Kathy was a sponsor.

Chapter 11

I forced my hand to unclench on the yellow playbill. Kathy had another connection to the murdered woman, but that didn't make her a murderess.

A strange cry drifted across the field. I twitched against the side of Hyperion's Jeep.

"An ostrich," Sandra said.

Swallowing, I turned the playbill so Sandra could see. "Did Kathy Landsford come to the theater much?"

The actress leaned forward, her back peeling off the wire fence, to see better. "Kathy? Oh, yeah. She loved watching rehearsals." She grinned. "She loved giving the director her opinions too."

So, Kathy *had* had access to the barn and maybe the air cannon. But had she had access to the pen knife that had killed Derek Benson?

"Did you ever see Lizzy with an antique pen knife?" I asked.

"No," Sandra said. "Why?"

"I thought she might have kept one here, at the theater."

She leaned back against the fence. The metal wires creaked beneath her weight. "If it was valuable, no way. We never left stuff here. All sorts of people come through—we're not the only actors using the barn. Things disappear, you know? Though sometimes that was just Lizzy."

"Do you mean Lizzy was a thief?" I asked, shocked.

"No, no," she said quickly. "Lizzy'd borrow props to take home for her photo shoots. But one time, the director caught her in the theater going at it hot and heavy with some guy. She was furious Lizzy would let a stranger inside. I mean, *he* could have been stealing the stuff for all we knew."

"Who was the guy?" I asked.

Sandra's full lip curled. "He ran off before the director could get much of a look at him. Typical Lizzy to pick someone who'd leave her holding the bag."

"And the, er, photoshoots?"

Gramps and Hyperion emerged from the red barn. Baranko followed them, wiping his hands on the front of his trench coat.

Sandra grinned. "Her ankle pics were brilliant," she said. "Show a little petticoat, and bam, the money pours in. Wish I'd thought of it."

"And the director didn't mind Lizzy borrowing the props?"

"Lizzy always brought them back undamaged. She just didn't always ask first."

"Do you know if there was an antique pen knife ever used as a prop?" Was this the answer? Did it all come down to the theater and Kathy?

"A real one?" She shook her head. "No way. All the knives in the prop room are rubber. The barn owner is terrified of liability."

Baranko gave a shout, and the two of us looked toward the barn. The detective stopped outside its wide doors and shook his fist in our direction. Even from this distance I could see his face was scarlet.

"What about an air cannon?" I asked quickly, edging toward the Jeep's door. "Was that ever used as a prop?"

Sandra smiled. "Not as a prop, but for special effects. We used it in the Scottish play which shall not be named."

I wrinkled my forehead. *Scottish play...?* "You mean, *Macbeth*?"

"Don't say the name! It's bad luck."

"Seriously? Mac—?"

She winced.

"Sorry," I said, contrite. "You were saying what about the air cannon?"

"One of the actors used an air cannon from behind the curtain to blow out Macbeth's candle. 'Out, out, brief candle!'"

"Stop talking," Baranko shouted, storming closer.

"Nice meeting you." Hastily, I climbed into the back of the Jeep. "Bye."

Baranko paused, glaring. Sandra edged farther away against the fence. Then he turned back, passing my grandfather and Hyperion, and retreating inside the barn.

I relaxed against the seat. I didn't know what Baranko could do to me for chatting with Sandra. But I preferred not to find out.

Gramps and Hyperion joined me in the Jeep.

"How'd it go?" I asked them.

"Since we arrived after the fact," Hyperion said, shutting his door, "we couldn't tell them anything."

Gramps grunted and pulled his seatbelt across his bulging stomach.

"I talked to the actress who found Lizzy." I handed Gramps the yellow playbill. "She said it looked like Lizzy had been shot with an antique gun."

"A dueling pistol?" Hyperion asked.

"Sounded like it."

My grandfather studied the playbill. His jaw worked silently. "What's this?"

"Did you know Kathy was sponsoring *Sense and Sensibility*?" I asked in a low voice.

"She may have mentioned it," he said. "Why?"

"She had access to the barn," I said. "Apparently, she liked to watch the rehearsals." Dread spooled in my gut. *The theater, the air cannon, Lizzy.*

Kathy.

"Kathy wasn't there today," Gramps said. "She couldn't have killed Lizzy." He cleared his throat.

I grimaced. "We don't know where Kathy was after the shooting in our parking lot."

My grandfather folded his arms, rumpling his tan jacket. "Yes, we do. She was at the police station. A detective told me she insisted on going there with him to make a formal report. Then she ran into the chief of police, who's a friend, and they had coffee in his office. The two were still in there when the station got the call about Lizzy." He stared through the windshield.

Another one of those strange cries floated from the far-off stand of Eucalyptus trees. My scalp prickled.

I shook my head. "Maybe she could have—"

"The director saw Lizzy and another actress arrive at one-thirty," Hyperion said. "That's about when you three came into my office shouting about getting shot at. Kathy's out."

"Besides," Gramps said, "Kathy couldn't have shot at us in the parking lot. You need to get off that track. Someone murdered two people. Lizzy was..." He shook his head.

"Kathy could have had an accomplice," I said stubbornly. "I mean, the accomplice could have taken the shot, making her look like a target rather than a suspect."

"Why are you so determined to make Kathy the villain?" Gramps asked.

"I'm not," I said. "I'm just trying to logic this out. But it didn't sound like Lizzy would have kept something as valuable as that pen knife here at the theater, so it doesn't matter if Kathy had access anyway."

"In other words, we've got nothing." Hyperion started the Jeep.

I folded my arms. "Not nothing. We've learned things were going missing at the theater."

"But if the pen knife wasn't at the theater," Gramps said, "that's got nothing to do with the murder."

"But there was an air cannon," I said. "They used it in Macbeth to blow out a candle behind the scenes."

"Was it stolen?" Hyperion pulled forward, and we bumped down the dirt drive.

"I don't know," I admitted. "Baranko interrupted."

"Kathy didn't kill anyone." My grandfather's jaw set.

"How can you be sure?" I asked. "If she had an accomplice—"

He twisted in his seat, his expression explosive. "Because I'm a better judge of character than—" He clamped his jaw shut and faced front.

I scrubbed my hand over my face. I'd gone too far. Why *did* I want Kathy to be the villain so badly?

"You likely are a better judge of character than me," I said quietly. I'd made catastrophic mistakes when we'd been starting up the tearoom. Gramps had helped me through most of them.

Hyperion's shoulders hunched. He cleared his throat.

"That's not what I was going to say," Gramps said in a low voice.

I didn't respond. We jounced over a pothole and drove in silence back to Beanblossom's. Hyperion vanished into his office. Gramps removed his checked hat, sat at the counter, and ordered tea and a roast beef sandwich, with a side of his horseradish. I got back to work.

Though the tearoom was packed, my staff knew their jobs. I felt a little in the way as I pitched in in the kitchen, so I went to chat with customers at their tables. A depressing number of them wanted to talk about the murder and the ghost.

"I'm very psychic." Mrs. McCarron adjusted the napkin in the lap of her floral-print dress. Though her hair was sleek and white, she was one of those women of indeterminate age. She could have been forty-five or sixty.

"Oh?" I pursed my lips, wary.

She leaned closer. "I sense a disturbed presence," she whispered.

"That's probably just me."

She blinked, then laughed ruefully. "Oh, Abigail, I apologize. You were *there*. The murder wasn't entertainment or intrigue for you. It was a bloody mess, I imagine. I'm sorry you had to go through that."

I smiled briefly. "Thanks. I'm sorry Mr. Benson's friends and relatives are going through it." Though it seemed Derek hadn't had many of either. Razzzor had tracked down an elderly aunt in Oregon—Derek's only relative.

Mrs. McCarron murmured more apologies, and I offered her a refill on her tea, which she declined. I returned to the white quartz counter and wiped it down with a damp cloth.

"I'm a better judge of character than I was when I was young," Gramps said in a low voice. He shifted his cabby hat further from his place.

"You couldn't have been so bad at it." I smiled. "You married Grandma."

He hesitated. "Right. The point is, you've got me beat. Your judgment is solid. Maybe I'm not seeing everything I should with Kathy. But I'm not in love with her. She's just an interesting friend I'd like to know better."

"Then you should." And I shouldn't have gotten on his case about Kathy. I just didn't want him to get hurt. I also didn't want to treat him like a child.

But I couldn't tell him either of those things. So, I smiled, and poured him more tea, and walked away to the kitchen to get him a roast beef sandwich.

Chapter 12

People say worrying about what might happen is a mistake. I call it emergency preparedness.

There'd been no way to prepare for a man being murdered in my tearoom. But I feared I could have stopped what had happened to Lizzy, and my stomach tightened.

Tossing the rag on the counter, I strode to Hyperion's office door. The twinkle lights faded as I approached. Frowning, I knocked. It had to be an electrical glitch. The building's electrical system hadn't been updated since the seventies.

"Come in," Hyperion called. The lights brightened.

I walked inside, closing the door behind me. Hyperion sat in his throne-like chair. A man in green stood motionless in one corner, as if lying in wait. I started at the apparition then exhaled.

It was Hyperion's green jacket, hanging from the coat tree in the corner. For a moment, it had looked like a man in green.

I made a face. *Who's buying into the mass hysteria now?* "I've been thinking—"

"Does your head hurt?" Hyperion asked without looking up from his laptop.

"Martin Carlton could have shot at us and had time to kill Lizzy."

Hyperion sat back in his red velvet chair and met my gaze. "As they say in improv, 'Yes, and...?'"

I slapped my hand to my chest. "You do improv?" Hyperion having a secret life wasn't as bad as Gramps having one. Except nothing Hyperion did was secret. He loved telling anyone who'd listen about his latest adventures.

"I did. In high school. I wasn't born this quick witted, you know. Improv."

I shook myself. *Moving on.* "We need to find out if he's got an alibi for Lizzy's murder. He certainly had reason to kill Derek."

"Being passed over for promotion?" He raised an eyebrow.

"If Martin was counting on that promotion, if he'd been led to believe it was his, it could have pushed him over the edge. It's why companies like to fire people on Fridays—to give them the weekend to cool off."

Hyperion checked his watch. "It's four o'clock. Don't you have a tearoom to run?"

"Yes, the third seating's about to start, but this is more important."

He blinked. "Okaaaay."

"It takes twenty minutes to get from here to the Ostrich Theater. Lizzy was killed some time before two o'clock. If Martin took a shot at us at one-thirty, he could have made it there in time to kill Lizzy."

Hyperion leaned his head back. He studied the white ceiling for a long moment then nodded. "Let's talk to Martin."

We drove in Hyperion's Jeep to Benson Investments, a discreet, one-story building with wooden shingles on the side. A Honda Civic pulled out in front of the building, and Hyperion swerved into the spot.

"The parking Gods favor me again." He grinned.

"You don't have to rub it in," I grumbled.

"Yes, I do. If you don't appreciate the gifts you're given, the universe will take them away."

We strolled through a Japanese tea garden-styled front yard. Hyperion opened one of the glass doors for me, and we walked inside. Bonsai trees lined the inset shelves behind the high, curving reception desk.

A woman in her mid-thirties, her eyes as red as her hair, looked up and sniffed. "May I help you?"

"We're here to see Martin Carlton," Hyperion said.

Her mouth pinched. "Do you have an appointment?"

"No," I said.

She plucked a phone from its receiver and pushed a button. "Mr. Carlton? Two people are here to see you."

I took a step backward. *Whoa.* She was actually letting us in? This was too easy.

The receptionist glanced at us and hung up. "What are your names?"

"Hyperion Night and Abigail Beanblossom," my partner said.

"You can go on back." She motioned with a pencil toward a beige-carpeted hallway to the left.

I hesitated. "Doesn't one normally, er—"

"Get the names *before* sending someone back?" the receptionist finished for me. Her smile was bitter. "Yes."

Hyperion braced an elbow on the high desk. "Carlton tough to work with?"

"You have no idea," she said. "And if you do, my condolences. He's in office 102."

"I'm sorry for your loss," I said in a low voice.

She stiffened. "Derek was a wonderful man."

Then she probably wouldn't give us any dirt on him. But she might on Martin Carlton. "And Martin?" I asked.

"I'm not a gossip. Try elsewhere." She swiveled her chair, putting her back to us.

That put me in my place. I followed Hyperion to room 102, just off the reception area. Hyperion knocked.

"Come in," Martin said.

The community liaison did not rise as we entered the cramped room. The wooden desk he sat behind was too big for the space, one of its shorter sides against a cream-colored wall. A narrow window overlooked the back of a camellia bush on the other side of the desk. Framed certificates filled the wall behind Martin.

One of Martin's brows lifted. "What are you two doing here?" His black suit jacket was buttoned, forcing the fabric to rumble over his midsection.

"We had some excitement after you left Beanblossom's," I said. "Someone took a shot at us. Did you see anyone acting suspiciously in the parking lot?"

"You too?" Nostrils flaring, he slapped shut the appointment book on his desk. "As I told Kathy, I don't have time to pay attention to people lurking in parking lots. I'm a busy man. And I resent you implying I might be the type of man to commit random shootings."

"It's unlikely it was random," Hyperion said.

His mouth pinched. "Nevertheless, the accusation is outrageous."

"We didn't accuse you of anything," Hyperion said coldly. "We only hoped you might have seen something."

"Well," he said, "I didn't."

"Did you come straight back to your office after you saw us?" I asked.

He straightened in his executive chair. "Why do you care?"

"Because someone murdered Lizzy Barnhart at the Ostrich Theater this afternoon," Hyperion said.

Martin's pinched face went white, then red. "And you're accusing me of killing that girl? I would never be associated with such a crime. Obviously, someone is plotting against Derek's company and trying to frame me."

"Who would do that?" Hyperion asked.

"How should I know? It's not my job to investigate crimes." His nose wrinkled.

"Are you implying that Derek's company has something to do with Lizzy?" I asked.

"She was an investor. Not a very happy one, but an investor nonetheless. Honestly, I thought *she* might have killed Derek. You should have heard her shrieking at him about the money she'd lost. But if you can't afford to lose, you can't afford to invest. He was a fool to let her put money into that project."

"Are any of the other people in your fan-fic group investors?" Hyperion asked.

"I can't tell you that."

But he'd told us about Lizzy. Murder had stripped away her privacy rights. "What time did you return to the office?"

He straightened in his chair and laid his hands flat upon the black appointment book. "I can assure you, no one at this office was involved in Derek's death, including myself. Have you seen my press statement?"

"Ah, no." Hyperion said.

Martin swiveled in his chair and plucked a sheet of paper from a black plastic OUT tray. He handed it across the wooden desk to Hyperion. "I think I worded it quite tactfully."

Hyperion scanned the paper. "Blah, blah... *In this time of trial, we continue to stand as a beacon of sound investment, under the wise guidance of our esteemed board. We are confident we shall prevail against this adversity.* Blah, blah, blah...

"*I assure all stakeholders, potential investors, and the community at large that our firm remains a paragon of ethical conduct,*" Hyperion continued. "Blah, blah. *We are cooperating fully with the authorities, and I am confident that the truth will exonerate us all.*"

"I resent all your blah, blah, blahs," Martin said. "I took a lot of time and care writing that."

"Yes," I gritted out. "But where were you between one-thirty and two p.m. today?"

"You have no right to ask me that," Martin said, shrill. "You're not the police."

"Would you prefer to talk to the police?" I asked. He'd be talking to them whether he preferred it or not if Kathy had told Baranko her suspicions.

"The police?" Martin quailed behind his desk, the folds in his black suit jacket deepening. "Why would they want to talk to me again? I'm a man of integrity."

"You're a man who was at the scene of a shooting and at least one murder," I snapped. "Where were you?"

"I was here, of course. I came straight back. Ask the receptionist if you don't believe me."

"Which one?" I asked.

"There's only one receptionist," he said.

My jaw tightened. I'd bet he didn't even know the woman's name. "And her name is...?"

"What does it matter what her name is?" Martin snapped. "She's a receptionist, she's at her desk, and I'll instruct her to answer your questions if she gives you any trouble. In fact, let's ask her now."

Martin reached for his desk phone and pressed a button. His hand trembled, clutching the receiver. There was a faint, buzzing sound.

"Yes?" the receptionist asked over the intercom.

"What time did I return from lunch today?" Martin asked.

"Around two," she said, "I think. Why?"

"None of your business." Martin hung up. "There. Satisfied?"

There was no way Martin could have made it to the theater and back by two o'clock, or even around two o'clock. He must have returned to his office directly from Beanblossom's.

"One more question," I said. "Did you arrange for Derek to be at the séance Sunday night?"

He straightened. "I did."

"Why?"

Martin patted his dark hair. "Derek didn't trust the results we were getting from our marketing firm. He wanted to talk to the TalesTrove.com clients himself."

"So he came to a séance," I said, disbelieving.

He rolled his eyes. "Well, there *was* that letter."

"Right." Hyperion nodded. "Thanks."

"Thanks for nothing," Martin said, voice rising. "How dare you come here? I've been accused today of murder, of attempted murder... If any of this makes it into the press, I'll sue you for libel."

My heart plunged, pity evaporating my disgust. Martin was pompous and silly, but he was also terrified... because of me.

Chapter 13

THE WORST LIES ARE the ones we tell ourselves.

I'd told myself I was only questioning a suspect, but I'd been bullying Martin. I'd told myself I wasn't treating my grandfather like a child, but I had been. His relationship with Kathy was his business, not mine.

I didn't like myself for any of it. I hadn't liked myself last night, tossing and turning alone in my bed. And I didn't like myself this morning.

I scanned the sea of gray and white heads seated around the tearoom's tables. My customers probably included their fair share of Kathys—hardened, tough, smart. But some of my most challenging customers, when I'd taken time to get to know them, had become my staunches allies and friends.

"Abigail?" a man said loudly.

I started, jerking my elbow off the white quartz counter.

Archer strode toward me in his yachting outfit. The older man adjusted his ascot. Chandelier light glimmered off his silvery hair. "Is it true Derek Benson's ghost is haunting the tearoom?"

"How should I know? I don't have a hotline to the otherworld."

"Is there a haunting?"

"Who told you there was?"

"Oh, please." He waved his hand negligently beside his wrinkled face. "Everyone's talking about it."

"Then why ask me?" I asked grumpily.

"You know... a ghost *would* be good for business."

I'm ashamed to admit I had considered that. These days, the right kind of ghost was a marketing plus. "It might be, if there *is* a ghost, and I can't be certain of that."

"Ah-ha!" He thrust a finger at me. "So, you've seen something too."

"Not seen, no."

"Felt? Smelled? Heard?"

"Archer..." I growled.

"Oh, don't be such a stick in the mud. You must know that the whole point of the paranormal is you *can't* prove it." He smoothed the front of his blue blazer. "But I appreciate your honesty. Now, did the haunted happenings begin the night of the murder?"

I slipped my hands into my apron pockets. "I'm not sure how to answer that."

"A simple yes or no would suffice."

"Archer... The murder was horrible." The understatement made me cringe. Murder was indescribably awful. We had one shot at life, to make it something glorious or throw away. But that was our choice. Someone had taken Derek's.

Archer patted my shoulder. "I know dear, murder always is. Most of humanity is rotten to the core. It's knowing that there are good people like you and your grandfather that keep me going. But the *ghost*?"

"Staff began reporting spooky things happening the next day."

But I'd sensed something *before* the murder, that odd coldness. My hands grew warm in my apron pockets, and I pulled them free. If there was something supernatural happening—*did* I actually believe that?—I couldn't be certain it was Derek's ghost.

"You could have another séance, find out, and close the last one properly," he wheedled.

"No," I said. "No more séances." *Although...*

"I've got a friend who's a *real* medium. I can invite her to the tearoom, keep it casual, and see what she says?"

"Thanks, but we've got Hyperion."

"My medium friend says some entities can be tough to dislodge," he warned. "You can't just wing it."

"Please don't write an article about Derek's ghost haunting the tearoom. It's too soon. He's got—" I thought of that receptionist. "He had people who cared about him. They don't want to read that. It's cruel."

He rolled his eyes and loosed a huff. "Fine. Be that way. I can hold the article... for now."

My muscles unbunched. "Thanks, Archer. You're a good egg."

"I am not," he said, indignant. "I'm a newspaper man living in the hell of an AI world." He pivoted and stormed from the tearoom. The bell over the blue front door jangled in his wake.

Kathy strode through the slowly closing door, the hems of her ivory wool cloak flaring around her hips. She scanned the tearoom, glowered, and walked to the counter, her heels clicking on the faux-wood floor.

The older woman set her cream-colored clutch on the counter and sat across from me. "We need to talk."

What now? I glanced around the tearoom. It was nearly noon, and the diners from our eleven o'clock seating were sitting back in their chairs, relaxing with their tea. "How can I help you?"

"You can stop babying your grandfather, for starters."

My eyes narrowed. "I don't baby him."

"Oh? You've been trying to keep him away from the murder investigation."

"Unsuccessfully," I said dryly. "He's a grown man, and he does what he wants."

She sniffed. "Then why try?"

Because I didn't want to lose him, and I didn't trust Kathy. But it *had* been wrong of me to try to keep him from charging into the investigation. Gramps wanted to live his best life with the years he had left. He deserved that.

"Do you know how you've hurt him?" she asked. "Treating him like... like... an old person."

I jerked my apron into place around my hips. Why is it extra insulting when someone tells you you've been wrong, *after* you've already come to the same conclusion? "I shouldn't have done it." And I *would* apologize.

Kathy relaxed a little on the barstool. "You don't like me very much." She tossed her head, her diamond earrings swaying.

"I think you act like a bully." I plucked a white teacup from beneath the counter, filled a strainer, and poured her a cup of Empress tea.

She watched me, took the cup I offered, took a sip. "*Act like*? You mean you believe deep down I'm not really a bully?" One corner of her lipsticked mouth curled derisively.

I shrugged. "Does it matter? For the rest of the world, we are how we behave, no matter what's going on inside us."

And maybe the same was true for me. Maybe it didn't matter if I worried about my grandfather. Maybe what mattered was what I did about it.

"And you don't want me bullying your grandfather," Kathy said.

I met her gaze. "He knows what he wants in his life. My grandfather can make his own decisions. And he won't be bullied."

"Good." She nodded. "Because I'd like to see more of him. And I'd think less of him if he allowed me to push him around. He hasn't, by the way."

My gaze clouded, and I frowned. I'd never known Gramps to date, and I wondered now why he hadn't. Because of me? But I'd been on my own for years now.

I exhaled slowly. Whatever the reason, if Gramps could change, then maybe I could too. But damn, it was a long process. I felt like I was bumbling in circles. Or maybe spirals, learning a little, repeating a different version of the same pattern, then learning a little more.

"But I don't let people stand in my way," she warned.

"And you think I might?" I shook my head. "What goes on between you and Gramps is between you and Gramps."

Kathy studied me through narrowed, emerald eyes. "And what about you?" she asked.

"What about me?"

"What have you decided?"

The bell over the blue front door jingled, a pair of women leaving. A cold draft raised gooseflesh on my arms.

A *séance*... "Why don't you take that coat off and stay awhile?" I said slowly. "It must be hot, and we could use your help."

She cocked her head. "Oh? For what?"

"For closing the séance. The staff thinks we let in a... ghost when we ended it so abruptly."

"You want to close the séance?" Kathy snorted. "Why on earth should I attend? Why should any of us? I presume you're going to reenact the murder. Isn't that a little too Agatha Christie?"

Behind the counter, my hands spasmed. *Darn it.* I *was* being too obvious. But I've found that fake confidence goes a long way, so I raised my chin. "You'll come because my grandfather will be there. The others will come because you're there."

And then we'd catch a killer.

Chapter 14

"No," Hyperion said. "You're the dead man. I'm the séance facilitator. You need to sit in the chair to the right."

Baranko glared at my partner. "I don't need to do anything." But he shifted over to the seat Hyperion pointed at. I exhaled slowly. The detective was annoyed, but at least he'd come.

Did I say annoyed? I meant furious. But I didn't think his rage was directed at us. Two murders under his watch within a week had heated him to a roiling boil.

"I'll take Lizzy's seat." I sat beside the detective, my knees brushing the tablecloth. The empty tables around us looked ghostly beneath their white tablecloth.

The tearoom was closed, the chandeliers glimmering. We'd shoved the other tables a little away from ours, like we had the night of Derek's murder. It was seven-fifteen, and the street outside the tearoom windows was shrouded in twilight gloom.

"Everyone else," Hyperion said, "sit where you were before."

Kathy and my grandfather sat, Gramps beating Martin to pulling out her chair. Martin, dressed like a funeral director, scowled.

Giorgi, in peacock colors, was slower to take his chair, making a business of pulling it away from the table. From the look Hyperion was giving it, I guessed Giorgi's suit was designer.

"We're really doing this?" Martin gripped the back of the wooden chair with both hands. "Having a do-over of the séance? Because even if the dead could talk, I'm not sure they should." He glanced at Kathy. "This is more than a little outside my comfort zone."

"I suspect it's outside everyone's comfort zone," Kathy said testily, her silvery blouse shimmering beneath the chandelier's light. "*Especially* people who outsource their thinking to AI."

Martin's mouth pinched. "I did not use—"

"And yes, *we* are doing this," she continued, "and it's not a do-over. We're closing the portal."

The socialite had exchanged today's heels for flats and her dangly diamonds for studs, as if readying for trouble. Her ivory coat hung like a ghost from the coat tree by the blue front door.

Baranko grunted. "Sit down."

"Fine." Martin sat, nostrils quivering. "But let's do this with respect and civility. No jump scares or sudden shocks, please. My heart's taken enough dealing with city council meetings."

"Not to mention Lizzy and Derek's murders." Giorgi's smile was pained. He dragged back his chair with a scraping noise.

"I would have thought that went without saying," Martin said huffily.

"We'll keep the lights on this time," I said, and Kathy looked disappointed. But I didn't want to be stuck in the dark with this crew.

"Well?" Baranko barked.

"Relax," Hyperion intoned. "Visualize a protective globe of white light surrounding everyone at the table."

"It didn't protect Derek very well, did it?" Kathy asked, arch.

"The white light protects from dark *spiritual* forces," Hyperion said, "not people."

"Aren't they the same?" Gramps pushed his cabby hat aside on the table, rumpling the white cloth. "Let's stop this, Abigail. We all know we're not here to try to close any portals. We're here to figure out what happened that night."

"Exactly." Kathy folded her arms.

I sagged against the back of my wooden chair. Hyperion had planned some special effects to "encourage" free speaking. It would be a disappointment for Hyperion, but I was glad we didn't have to use them. I hadn't thought they'd work.

"All right." A cold draft touched the back of my neck, and I pulled the collar of my green blouse closer. I frowned at Hyperion. He seemed determined to pull his tricks. "Everyone at that séance had a reason to want Derek dead."

"Except for me and Abigail," Hyperion said hastily.

"I didn't have a motive," Gramps said.

"And my grandfather," I amended. "Derek secretly patented Giorgi's idea for a writing platform and cut him out of the business."

Giorgi folded his arms. "Old news."

"Derek passed Martin over for a long-promised promotion," I continued.

"I'd hardly kill someone over *that*," Martin said.

"Kathy and Derek were rivals for Giorgi's Jane Austen letter." I nodded to Kathy.

"As Martin said," Kathy sniffed, "I would hardly kill for that."

I cleared my throat. "Lizzy lost money on an investment with Derek—"

"And she's dead." The word dropped like a stone from Giorgi's mouth.

There was a long silence. Baranko glowered.

"Yes," I finally said, "it's unlikely Lizzy committed the crime. But she was an unwitting participant."

"What do you mean?" Kathy released her arms and leaned forward, resting them on the white tablecloth.

I adjusted my necklace. It wasn't often I got to play master detective. The role wasn't as fun as it looked on TV.

"I mean the evidence kept pointing to Lizzy," I said. "She was seated right beside Derek during the séance. The air cannon used to extinguish the candle came from her theater—"

"How do you know that?" Kathy leaned forward.

"I know," Baranko said. "The director confirmed it was one of their special effects devices."

"And the knife used to kill Derek belonged to her," Hyperion said.

"So, she killed herself." Martin grimaced. "She must have felt the walls closing in."

"Suicide. I can't believe it." Giorgi shook his head. "She was so… *alive*."

The chandeliers briefly dimmed. I glanced at Hyperion and shook my head slightly. *Enough.*

Baranko smiled, sharklike. "Oh, she didn't kill herself. Not with that dueling pistol."

"Why not?" Kathy asked.

"Because when someone was shooting at you three with the dueling pistol," Baranko said, "Miss Barnhart was already at the theater."

"What about Frank?" Giorgi motioned toward my grandfather.

"He's the only one who hasn't got a motive." Baranko stared from beneath lowered brows at my grandfather. "Though I don't believe your harmless-old-man schtick."

My grandfather shrugged. "I didn't say I was harmless."

"Was Lizzy killed because she knew too much?" Kathy tugged at the cuffs of her silvery blouse. Its billowy sleeves could hide a dueling pistol.

"Something like that," I said. "She recognized her antique pen knife the night of the séance. That's what had sent her fleeing to the bathroom—not Derek's death. And eventually, she realized there was only one person who could have taken it from her apartment. The same person who had access to the theater and its prop air cannon."

"A thief?" Martin asked.

"Her lover," Hyperion said. "Kathy, you were at the theater frequently—"

"I was *not* Lizzy's lover," she said hotly and glanced at my grandfather. "I like men."

"Did you ever see Lizzy there with a man?" Hyperion asked her.

"No," she said.

"Hold on," Giorgi said. "Didn't Frank say he had a friend at the local theater? That's where he borrowed his costume from. He had access. And he was sitting right next to Derek."

The chandeliers flickered. We all looked up.

I forced a smile. The electrical trick was more subtle than I'd expected from my partner, but I could tell the others weren't buying it.

"Uh, but he doesn't have a motive," Hyperion said.

"How do you know Frank wasn't Lizzy's sugar daddy?" Giorgi asked.

"Because I'm cheap," Gramps said.

"That's true." Hyperion bobbled his head.

"Please," Kathy huffed. "Frank would never."

An expression of mild regret crossed my grandfather's face.

"Means, motive and opportunity," I said hurriedly. "The pen knife was the means. All of you had a motive. As to opportunity, it took a lot of nerve for the killer to walk around us in the dark, stab Derek, then return to their chair."

"So?" Martin asked. "Who was it?"

"Stabbing someone is a bloody business," I said. "Literally. The killer would have gotten blood on their hands."

"Then it couldn't have been me," Martin said. "My hands were clean. You saw them."

"The killer couldn't be certain of wiping them perfectly clean in the dark," I said, "though I imagine the killer tried. But there was a simple fix for that."

Martin rose. "This is ridiculous. I have better things to do than—"

"Sit down," Baranko snarled.

Martin sat.

The lights flickered again, and I sighed heavily. I wished Hyperion really were psychic. Then he could read my thoughts: *knock it off with the lights.*

"The killer got around it by being one of the first people to *help.*" I put the final word in air quotes. "Everyone who tried to help Derek got blood on them. It was the perfect cover."

Giorgi's brows lowered. "Frank—"

"Not my grandfather," I said, voice hard. "You. You were Lizzy's secret boyfriend. You stole the pen knife from her apartment. You got her to let you into the theater through the back door. And she really wanted to talk to you yesterday, to ask about that knife."

"Ridiculous," Giorgi said. "You can't prove a thing."

"I think we can," Baranko said. "You sure you wiped all your prints from Miss Barnhart's apartment?"

Giorgi paled. "All right. I've been to her apartment. What of it?" He sneered. "Lots of men have been in and out of there."

My grandfather's eyes narrowed. "So that was it? You wanted revenge on Derek?"

"I've moved on from that business venture," Giorgi said. "It was years ago. Why would I kill Derek now?"

"Because Derek discovered your Jane Austen letter was a forgery," I said. It was a guess, but I thought it was a pretty good one.

Giorgi leapt to his feet. His chair tipped, clattering to the floor. "Ridiculous."

"There were matchsticks littered around one of the candles in your condo," I said. "That's where you were practicing with your air cannon, making sure you could hit your target."

"Sit down," Baranko said.

"Your father was a rare book restorer," I said. "You learned the trade from him. And according to Kathy, you have lovely penmanship."

She pressed a hand to her throat. "He *does*."

"You're a peacock," I told him. "Every time I've seen you since the night of the murder, you've worn bold colors. But that night, you wore black to hide the blood more easily. Oh, you had an excuse for the blood, and the police took your clothing anyway. But why ruin a good suit?"

"I can wear black if I want," Giorgi said sullenly.

"You *did* want revenge on Derek," I said. "You wanted to sucker him with that phony letter. Getting Kathy to bid up the price only sweetened the deal. But when Derek realized it was a fake, he confronted you. He wasn't a fan of Kathy, but he would have told her before she paid for a fake. As he told you at the séance, he never let things go. Little did he know, you were planning to kill him that very night."

Giorgi bolted for the front door. Baranko was faster.

Chapter 15

"The rehash of the séance was unnecessary." Baranko leaned against the kitchen's long, metal worktable. "The killer didn't confess."

"I thought the second séance would be more fun," Hyperion said thoughtfully. He bit into a currant scone.

"You overdid it playing with the lights," I said.

"I told you, it wasn't me." My partner pressed a hand to the front of his charcoal turtleneck. "I swear."

"Though I always wanted to summon the suspects for a final reveal," Baranko admitted, wistful.

So *that* was why the detective had agreed to the séance. I gave the reach-in refrigerator a final swipe and closed the lid.

Tonight was Friday, and the kitchen was clean. My boyfriend's plane should have landed by now, and Brik and I would be celebrating with our feet up on my coffee table at home. All was well with the world.

"She's right. Playing with the lights was overkill," the detective complained. "Did you really think anyone would fall for it?"

"For the fifteenth time," Hyperion said, "I didn't—"

There was a soft thud, and I jumped. On the floor, a metal ladle swayed on a black fatigue mat. It must have fallen from the metal counter. I scooped it up and set it on the long, metal worktable. *Ghosts. Ha.*

We *had* closed the portal, Hyperion, Gramps, Kathy and I, after everyone had left. My stomach quivered. Or at least, if there had been a portal, I *hoped* it was now closed.

We hadn't had any ghostly occurrences since that night, and the staff seemed satisfied. I glanced again at the ladle. Things fell off counters. No biggie.

Hyperion pressed his hand to his chest. "Detective Baranko, are you secretly supernatural curious?"

The big man's face flushed. "No. I just thought you'd be putting on a better show, that's all."

"Do you need a confession from Giorgi?" I straightened, my pulse accelerating. Giorgi had nursed his revenge against Derek for years. I didn't want someone like that on the streets—not when we might be his next target.

Baranko shook his head. "We got him. His fingerprints are in Ms. Barnhart's apartment and dressing room. We found the second dueling pistol in his condo. He's done."

The kitchen door swung open, and my grandfather ambled in. "You finished here?" He wore a mildly frayed brown business jacket and knit vest that I recognized from his days as a CPA.

"Just about," I said. "Detective Baranko was telling us that they have enough evidence to convict without Giorgi's confession."

"And the Jane Austen letter?" Gramps asked.

"We'll find an expert to go over it," the detective said. "There was a guy in Santa Cruz we thought we could use, but he couldn't be sure if it was a fake or not. There's a specialist the FBI uses in San Francisco. We'll get his opinion."

My hand spasmed on the damp washcloth. "Hold on. You mean, the letter might actually be real?" That would blow up our motive for murder. Not that Giorgi needed another. Being pushed out of the start-up was enough.

Baranko shrugged. "Real, fake, who cares? We got a murderer, and we didn't need your help." He glowered at Hyperion.

"What are you giving *me* the fish-eye for?" Hyperion pointed at me. "This is a partnership."

The detective grunted and strode from the kitchen. The door swung in his wake.

"He might not have needed us," Hyperion said, "but he agreed to the repeat séance."

Head cocked, I watched the door sway to a stop. Could Baranko be a romantic at heart?

Nah.

"What are you doing here?" I asked my grandfather.

He glanced at Hyperion. "I'm, uh, on my way to pick up Kathy."

"For a date?" My partner asked gleefully.

"I thought I'd bring some scones if you had any left over." Gramps turned his cabbie-style tweed hat in his hands.

"It *is* a date," Hyperion said.

Gramps jerked his head toward the door. "Can you give us a minute?"

"Sure, sure, sure." Hyperion bustled from the kitchen.

"And no listening at the door," Gramps bellowed.

I bit back a laugh. "What's up?"

"Razzzor called and told me there was no indication of foul play in the deaths of Kathy's husbands."

I stiffened. *Dammit.* I'd forgotten to call Razzzor off. "I'm sorry. I—"

"I was pretty mad at him, at first. But he told me background checks were normal in the dating world." He shook his head. "Things sure have changed since the last time I've been on a date."

I crumpled my hands in my apron. "Gramps, I asked Razzzor to check her out. I'm sorry."

"I know you did. But I'm glad. This new tech isn't all bad. Now I know she's in the clear. No indication of foul play."

I looked down at the black fatigue mat. That didn't mean there hadn't *been* any foul play. It just meant the police hadn't seen fit to investigate further.

I pulled out a white flat-pack box from beneath a counter. "Still, she lost two wealthy husbands."

"I'm not wealthy."

"And you want to risk it?" I raised an eyebrow.

"Yeah." He slapped his cap on his head. "I do."

I studied him. One of the buttons in his vest was in the wrong hole. His cap had a rakish tilt over his tufts of white hair. Gramps was Gramps, and some things would never change.

But we couldn't stay stuck in that past. He had to take the risk and jump in, and I had to take the risk and let go.

I opened a larger box that I'd packed and pulled out a scone with a pair of tongs. "I've never seen your fan-fic."

His round face went scarlet. "It's not professionally written."

"No one starts as a pro. We learn as we go along. That's the fun of it."

"Yeah, but—"

I brandished the tongs. "I'll trade scones and lemon curd for a peek?"

"You always give me scones anyway."

"And I'll keep Hyperion from squeezing you for intel on your date." It would be a challenge, mainly because I wanted intel on his upcoming date. But giving my grandfather his privacy was part of letting go, wasn't it?

My grandfather grinned. "Deal."

***

Author's Note:

File this under: "Where do I get my ideas?"

There's a lot of drama in real life, and especially in a massive storm.

When a category 5 storm hit the town I was using as a (very loose) model for San Borromeo in my Tea and Tarot mystery series, I felt I had to use it in my next book.

Thankfully, no one was killed in the real town of Capitola, but there was a lot of damage, especially to the businesses along the oceanfront.

The VERY good news is the storm damage has since been repaired, including the marvelous Capitola pier. It was inspiring to see how the real town pulled together, and I hope I captured some of that in my book.

The running themes of my cozy mysteries are hope, joy, and community. And though no one *enjoys* the hard times while they're happening, it's the hard times that can bring out the best in us.

I hope you enjoyed this novella!

Turn the page for Abigail's currant scone recipe and more fun from Beanblossom's Tea and Tarot!

Currant Scones

Ingredients:
- 2 C flour
- 1 1/3 C sugar
- 1 ½ tsp baking powder
- ½ tsp salt
- ½ C unsalted butter
- ½ C heavy whipping cream OR Italian sweet cream coffee creamer
- ½ C currants

Directions:
1. Preheat oven to 375 degrees F. Line baking sheet with parchment.
2. Place dry ingredients except for currants in food processor and pulse to combine.
3. Cut butter into pieces and add to dry ingredients.
4. Pulse until mixture resembles a coarse meal.
5. With processor on low, stream in cream or creamer.
6. Add currants and fold in with a big spoon.

7. Lightly knead dough with hands until it forms a rough ball. Do not over knead.

8. Divide dough into two sections and flatten into disks 1 ½" thick.

9. Cut into triangles, place on parchment about ½" apart.

10. Bake 14-18 minutes.

Beanblossom's Swag Shop!

Be a Beanblossoms Patron!
Would you like to sip tea from a Beanblossom's mug? Check out Kirsten's swag shop HERE.
By purchasing our hoodies, t-shirts, and mugs, you're backing the *Tea and Tarot* series. Your love for these books fuels future hilarious adventures!

More Kirsten Weiss

THE DOYLE WITCH MYSTERIES

In a mountain town where magic lies hidden in its foundations and forests, three witchy sisters must master their powers and shatter a curse before it destroys them and the home they love.

This thrilling witch mystery series is perfect for fans of Annabel Chase, Adele Abbot, and Amanda Lee. If you love stories rich with packed with magic, mystery, and murder, you'll love the Witches of Doyle. Follow the magic with the Doyle Witch trilogy, starting with book 1, *Bound*.

The Mystery School Series

The Doyle Witches have created a mystery school, and a woman starting over becomes a student of magic and murder…

This metaphysical mystery series is perfect for readers who love a good page-turner as well as the deeper questions that accompany life's transitions. These empowering books come with their own oracle app, the UnTarot, plus downloadable mystery school worksheets. The Doyle Witch magic continues, starting with book 1, *Legacy of the Witch*.

The Perfectly Proper Paranormal Museum Mysteries

When highflying Maddie Kosloski is railroaded into managing her small-town's paranormal museum, she tells herself it's only temporary… until a corpse in the museum embroils her in murders past and present.

If you love quirky characters and cats with attitude, you'll love this laugh-out-loud cozy mystery series with a light paranormal twist. It's perfect for fans of Jana DeLeon, Laura Childs, and Juliet Blackwell. Start with book 1, *The Perfectly Proper Paranormal Museum*, and experience these charming wine-country whodunits today.

The Tea & Tarot Cozy Mysteries

Welcome to Beanblossom's Tea and Tarot, where each and every cozy mystery brews up hilarious trouble.

Abigail Beanblossom's dream of owning a tearoom is about to come true. She's got the lease, the start-up funds, and the recipes. But Abigail's out of a tearoom and into hot water when her realtor turns out to be a conman... and then turns up dead.

Take a whimsical journey with Abigail and her partner Hyperion through the seaside town of San Borromeo (patron saint of heartburn sufferers). And be sure to check out the easy tearoom recipes in the back of each book! Start the adventure with book 1, *Steeped in Murder*.

The Wits' End Cozy Mysteries

Cozy mysteries that are out of this world...

Running the best little UFO-themed B&B in the Sierras takes organization, breakfasting chops, and a talent for turning up trouble.

The truth is out there... Way out there in these hilarious whodunits. Start the series and beam up book 1, *At Wits' End*, today!

Pie Town Cozy Mysteries

When Val followed her fiancé to coastal San Nicholas, she had ambitions of starting a new life and a pie shop. One broken engagement later, at least her dream of opening a pie shop has come true.... Until one of her regulars keels over at the counter.

Welcome to Pie Town, where Val and pie-crust specialist Charlene are baking up hilarious trouble. Start this laugh-out-loud cozy mystery series with book 1, *The Quiche and the Dead*.

A Big Murder Mystery Series

Small Town. Big Murder.

The number one secret to my success as a bodyguard? Staying under the radar. But when a wildly public disaster blew up my career and reputation, it turned my perfect, solitary life upside down.

I thought my tiny hometown of Nowhere would be the ideal out-of-the-way refuge to wait out the media storm.

It wasn't.

My little brother had moved into a treehouse. The obscure mountain town had decided to attract tourists with the world's largest collection of big things... Yes, Nowhere now has the world's largest pizza cutter. And lawn flamingo. And ball of yarn...

And then I stumbled over a dead body.

All the evidence points to my brother being the bad guy. I may have been out of his life for a while—okay, five years—but I know he's no killer. Can I clear my brother before he becomes Nowhere's next Big Fatality?

A fast-paced and funny cozy mystery series, start with Big Shot.

The Riga Hayworth Paranormal Mysteries

Her gargoyle's got an attitude.

Her magic's on the blink.

Alchemy might be the cure... if Riga can survive long enough to puzzle out its mysteries.

All Riga wants is to solve her own personal mystery—how to rebuild her magical life. But her new talent for unearthing murder keeps getting in the way...

If you're looking for a magical page-turner with a complicated, 40-something heroine, read the paranormal mystery series that fans of Patricia Briggs and Ilona Andrews call AMAZING! Start your next adventure with book 1, *The Alchemical Detective.*

Sensibility Grey Steampunk Suspense

California Territory, 1848.

Steam-powered technology is still in its infancy.

Gold has been discovered, emptying the village of San Francisco of its male population.

And newly arrived immigrant, Englishwoman Sensibility Grey, is alone.

The territory may hold more dangers than Sensibility can manage. Pursued by government agents and a secret society, Sensibility must decipher her father's clockwork secrets, before time runs out.

If you love over-the-top characters, twisty mysteries, and complicated heroines, you'll love the Sensibility Grey series of steampunk suspense. Start this steampunk adventure with book 1, *Steam and Sensibility.*

Introducing the UnTarot App: Step into the Enchantment of Kirsten Weiss's Mystery School Series!

EMBARK ON A JOURNEY that intertwines fiction and reality as you dive into the captivating world of Kirsten Weiss's upcoming Mystery School series. With the UnTarot app, you can wield the very cards the characters from the books utilize, tapping into a wellspring of ancient wisdom and boundless magic.

Imagine harnessing the power of the UnTarot cards to unlock hidden insights and unravel the threads of fate. With the UnTarot app, you gain access to a treasure trove of captivating readings and interpretations. As you explore this mystical experience, you'll be drawn into a world where the boundaries between fiction and reality blur.

- **Authentic Connection:** Immerse yourself in the enchanting ambiance of the Mystery School series. The UnTarot app faithfully captures the essence of the books, allowing you to connect with the characters and their adventures on a whole new level.

- **Ancient Wisdom, Modern Convenience:** The UnTarot app marries centuries-old divination techniques with cutting-edge technology, creating an accessible experience for both seasoned practitioners and curious novices.

- **Free Exploration**: Yes, you read that right! The UnTarot app is entirely FREE, ensuring that everyone can join in the magical journey of self-discovery, insight, and revelation.

Ready to embark on a journey that defies the boundaries of time and space? The UnTarot app beckons you to step into the wondrous world of Kirsten Weiss's Mystery School series. Download the UnTarot app and let the magic unfold before your very eyes!

Download the UnTarot app for FREE today and embrace the enchantment that awaits!

2:32
untarot.beezer.com
Install The UnTarot
https://untarot.beezer.com
ADD TO HOME SCREEN

About the Author

I BELIEVE IN FREE-WILL, and that we all can make a difference. I believe that beauty blossoms in the conscious life, particularly with friends, family, and strangers. I believe that genre fiction has become generic, and it doesn't have to be.

My current focus is my new Mystery School series, starting with *Legacy of the Witch*. Traditionally, women's fiction refers to fiction where a woman—usually in her midlife—is going through some sort of dramatic change. A lot of us do go through big transitions in midlife. We get divorced or remarried. The kids leave the nest. Our bodies change. The midlife crisis is real—though it manifests in different ways—as we look back on where we've been, where we're going, and the time we have left.

Now in my mid-fifties, I've spent more time thinking about the big "meaning of life" issues. It seemed like approaching those issues through witch fiction, and through a fictional mystery school, would be a fun and a useful way for me to work out some of these ideas in my own head—about change and letting go, faith and fear, and love and longing.

After growing up on a diet of Nancy Drew, Sherlock Holmes, and Agatha Christie, I've published over 60 mysteries—from cozies to supernatural suspense, as well as an experimental fiction book on Tarot. Spending over 20 years working overseas in international development, I learned that perception is not reality, and things are often not what they seem—for better or worse.

There isn't a winter holiday or a type of chocolate I don't love, and some of my best friends are fictional.

Sign up for my **newsletter** for exclusive stories and book updates. I also have a read-and-review tea via **Booksprout** and I'm looking for honest and thoughtful reviews! If you're interested, download the **Booksprout app**, follow me on Booksprout, and opt-in for email notifications.

bookbub.com/profile/kirsten-weiss

goodreads.com/author/show/5346143.Kirsten_Weiss

facebook.com/kirsten.weiss

instagram.com/kirstenweissauthor/

youtube.com/@KirstenWeiss-Writer?sub_confirmation=1

Other misterio press books

Please check out these other great *misterio press* series:
Karma's A Bitch: Pet Psychic Mysteries
by Shannon Esposito
Multiple Motives: Kate Huntington Mysteries
by Kassandra Lamb
The Metaphysical Detective: Riga Hayworth Paranormal Mysteries
by Kirsten Weiss
Dangerous and Unseemly: Concordia Wells Historical Mysteries
by K.B. Owen
Murder, Honey: Carol Sabala Mysteries
by Vinnie Hansen
Payback: Unintended Consequences Romantic Suspense
by Jessica Dale
Buried in the Dark: Frankie O'Farrell Mysteries
by Shannon Esposito
To Kill A Labrador: Marcia Banks and Buddy Cozy Mysteries
by Kassandra Lamb
Lethal Assumptions: C.o.P. on the Scene Mysteries
by Kassandra Lamb
Never Sleep: Chronicles of a Lady Detective Historical Mysteries
by K.B. Owen
Bound: Witches of Doyle Cozy Mysteries

by Kirsten Weiss
At Wits' End Doyle Cozy Mysteries
by Kirsten Weiss
Steeped In Murder: Tea and Tarot Mysteries
by Kirsten Weiss
The Perfectly Proper Paranormal Museum Mysteries
by Kirsten Weiss
Big Shot: The Big Murder Mysteries
by Kirsten Weiss
Steam and Sensibility: Sensibility Grey Steampunk Mysteries
by Kirsten Weiss
Full Mortality: Nikki Latrelle Mysteries
by Sasscer Hill
ChainLinked: Moccasin Cove Mysteries
by Liz Boeger
Maui Widow Waltz: Islands of Aloha Mysteries
by JoAnn Bassett

Plus even more great mysteries/thrillers in the *misterio press* bookstore

Made in the USA
Middletown, DE
11 July 2025